THE BODEGA WAR

And Other Tales from Western Lore

THE BODEGA WAR

AND OTHER STORIES FROM WESTERN LORE

Hector H. Lee

CAPRA PRESS

SANTA BARBARA

1988

Cover illustration by Judy Sutcliffe
Design and typography by Jim Cook
SANTA BARBARA, CALIFORNIA

LIBRARY OF CONGRESS CATALOGING-IN-PUBLICATION DATA
The Bodega War: and other stories from western lore
compiled by Hector H. Lee.
ISBN 0-88496-279-2 (pbk.) $8.95   p. cm.
1. Western stories.   2. California—Fiction.   I. Lee, Hector, 1908- .
PS648.W4T35   1988   813'.0874'08—dc19   87-28814 CIP

Published by
CAPRA PRESS
Post Office Box 2068
Santa Barbara, California 93120

*I owe sincere thanks to those tolerant friends who
have helped me one way or another to nurture these
stories to their present condition of maturity:
Homer and Sylph Bronson, Robert Coleman,
Barbara Knight, Pattie Lewin, Marjorie McLain,
Don Roberson, Margaret Rosenfeld,
Leslie and Lora Rowe, Dale and Harriet Winn,
Field and Roma Winn.*

*And thanks also to my son David Lee
and of course, as always, to Ina.*

CONTENTS

A NOTE TO THE READER

HERE ARE SOME stories drawn from California's legendary past and from my observations of people and events during a lifetime in the American West. Some have their roots in historical facts; Death Valley Scotty was a very real and colorful person, Remme did make his epic ride from Sacramento to Portland, and Tamsen Donner actually had to reach her painful and final decision in that snowbound camp on the wrong side of the high Sierras in 1847. But for the most part these tales are to be viewed as fiction.

As a storyteller for more years than I can decently lie about, I have found that most people enjoy reading or hearing stories involving a character worth knowing, a theme worth remembering, and a situation fraught with enough suspense to make the narrative worth finishing. I hope you find such qualities here. Some of these tales have been rendered orally by professional storytellers of my acquaintance and have pleased audiences interested in the telling as an accomplished art. "Lucia and Old Lace," "Chief Little Sitting Bear," and "The Mink Creek Ghost" have already found their way into the repertoires of such storytellers.

At the end of the collection you will find a section providing critical commentary on each story. Teachers may find this useful. But if you already know more than you want to know about the types of stories and the techniques involved in writing them, you can ignore these analyses; you may not agree with them, anyway. They were written by, let us say, an anonymous and somewhat academic critic whose only aim has been to help clarify my intentions—which were quite honorable, I assure you.

Finally, I do not pretend that these add up to being a representative portrayal of the Old West, the Far West, or any other kind of West. Simply, they all have their setting somewhere west of the Rocky Mountains, and they offer glimpses of life there both past and present. They were written primarily for enjoyment, yours and mine.

—Hector H. Lee

THE BODEGA WAR

And Other Tales from Western Lore

The horrible, colorless, unrelenting ghost of death . . .

Tamsen Donner's Decision

THE SNOWSTORM HAD abated and a faint hint of sunlight was beginning to penetrate the gray mist that smothered the valley, but Tamsen Donner knew the respite was only temporary. Already more heavy black clouds were rolling in from the north, indicating that another storm was on its way. A renewed hope of rescue, however, was at last approaching in the person of William Eddy, whom she recognized as he came down the trail toward her. He had been a member of the stranded wagon train and had gone ahead to get help to save his wife and children. Following him were two strangers who, with the assistance of her own faithful hired men, Baptiste and Clark, would be ample manpower to deliver herself and her three little girls from impending death, and start them on the path to freedom and a new life.

And yet Tamsen was not ready to go. After some brief preliminary conversation Eddy came directly to the vital question: how soon would she be ready to leave and start the perilous trek over the snowpacked mountain barrier to the safety of Sutter's Fort? To his surprise Tamsen held back.

"Missis Donner, it's time for you to make up your mind what you're goin' to do," Eddy said bluntly. Clearly her indecision annoyed him. "We can't wait no longer. We can take you and the

13

girls with us, and there's a pretty good chance that we'll make it over the mountains before this next storm comes in."

For Tamsen Donner these words which she had waited so long to hear had come too late. And yet at this moment with mocking irony they had come too soon. "You know I can't go now and leave my sick husband alone in this Godless place," she sighed, and tears came to her tired eyes.

"But he's just about—I have to say this, ma'am—but your husband is about to go under at any time now." William Eddy did not want to be cruel, but for too long he had been in the midst of pain and death; for him grief had become commonplace, and he had seen too many loved ones abandoned when they were no longer able to survive. "You can't save him," he added, "but you can save yourself and the children."

"Just one more day or two," the desperate woman pleaded. "He can't last more than a day or two. I know that. But he needs me here by him. Please?"

"I'm afraid we can't do that, ma'am. It's now or never." Eddy's meaning was plain enough. He had come to rescue Tamsen Donner and her children from the snowbound prison in which they had been struggling so long for their very lives against the enemies that had claimed in death so many of their wagon train company— starvation, sickness, despair, and the unrelenting cold. Now the hour of deliverance was at hand, and she knew that to delay any longer would be to court certain death in the new storm that was already threatening.

Why had God forced her to make such a fatal choice? He had led her to this ultimate crossroad from which there could be no turning back. One way meant that she must give up her little children to the care of strangers, never to see them again. For a devoted mother this was unthinkable; but to choose the other path meant enduring the anguish that must tear at the heart of a woman who would abandon her dying husband, never to care for him again in life or death. Who among the living could ever know with what aching conscience she must search her memories, her sacred vows, and her steadfast faith to make such a decision?

Somehow she must find the courage to choose between her love and loyalty to an old man, on the one hand, with her own certain death as a result; or on the other hand the promise of life and the rewarding duties of motherhood, with the dream of protecting her little girls from the hazards of life in a strange land. In the urgent space of two or three hours, alone, here in that snowbound shelter on the wrong side of the towering white peaks of the Sierra Nevada Mountains, she must decide. William Eddy could wait no longer for an answer.

"Can't you wait just another day or two?" Tamsen repeated her plea. "I can't leave my husband. I can't just walk away from him when he is dying, and I can't send the girls out alone." She was fighting for time, now, in the hope that fate would take the decision out of her hands. With her help and protection along the way, her three little girls were strong enough to endure the hazardous trek through the snow that choked the passage over the high mountains to the safety of Sutter's Fort in California. Things were coming to a conclusion at the Donner camp on Alder Creek, and in two or three days at the most she could leave with a clear conscience. Uncle Jake Donner had died of starvation and pneumonia, and they had learned to their horror that Louis Keseberg had found his remains and had eaten his arms and legs. Yesterday Aunt Betsy had died, and her frozen body was lying under a canvas at the Donner camp. In her folded arms Tamsen had gently placed the old family Bible in which she had written a final note: "Elizabeth Donner, wife of Jacob Donner, age 45, died March 4, 1847."

"No, we can't wait," Eddy insisted. "You can see there's another storm comin', and the others over at the lake are ready. We've got to go now." Tamsen understood the urgency of the situation, but she needed time, just a little more time. "What about the other children?" she asked. "Did they get out all right?" The older children of Elizabeth and Jacob had gone out with an earlier rescue party, but their baby, little Sammy, not more than a year old, could not be taken, and he was now near death.

"I think they got away all right. They'll make it." And sensing the depth of her concern which lay behind the question, Eddy asked, "How's your husband now?"

"I just told you." Tamsen's voice choked, and the words were hard to say. "He's about gone," she said, and her lips trembled. Her husband, George, was lying in a coma from the infection in his hand, which had taken over his whole arm, and he was sinking fast. Just a few more days and she would be released from her responsibilities at Alder Creek.

"I wish we could wait, Miz Donner, but you can see we can't."

Tamsen's thoughts flashed to the ordeal of Virginia Reed, whose situation was not unlike her own. Mrs. Reed had gone out along with her older children a week ago with another party, but her two youngest—little Patty, only eight years old, and Tommy who was but three—could not keep up and had been forced to return to the Murphy cabin at the lake. It took courage for Virginia to leave them behind, but at least she had the hope that another relief party was on its way to rescue them. Jim Reed, who had reached California first and alone after his earlier banishment from the wagon train, had organized several searching parties to bring what food they could carry and to guide the survivors out to safety. He had been able to rescue his abandoned children and take them along with a few others out to safety. They were probably in California by now.

"Tell you what I'll do, Miz Donner," Eddy said. He realized the tragic finality of the poor woman's decision as well as the inevitability of it. "You've got three or four hours before dark. We want to leave come daylight tomorrow morning, and here's the best I can do for you. I'll leave Cady and Stone here with you, and you've got Clark and Baptiste to help out. If you decide to come we'll take you. Or if you just send the young'ns out, Stone and Cady can take them over to the lake, and if they can keep up they can go with the others. If they can't, they'll get left, and that's the long and the short of it. Clark can stay with you here, and if things clear up for you, him and you can come out later—if there's another rescue, which I can't say for certain. Clark and Baptiste can make it out anyway, no matter what." Having said all there was to say, Eddy turned and left. The four men, Stone, Cady, Clark, and Baptiste, busied themselves burying Aunt Betsy's body in as deep a hole as they could dig in the ice-packed snow, and Tamsen Donner sat down on the cot where her dying husband lay. She wondered whom she could trust among these men who were supposed to help her. Young Jean Baptiste, the Donners' hired man who had come with them to drive one of their wagons, was loyal and dependable. Nicholas Clark would be all right; he was a robust, round-faced young man who seemed eager to face the challenge of the situation. Stone and Cady, however, were a different sort. They made her think of lean and hungry wolves stalking their prey. And yet she had to trust them; they were her only hope.

She touched her husband's forehead and it was hot under her gentle hand; the fever was still there. The three little girls, who had remained in huddled silence during the meeting with Eddy, now came close to her with fear in their eyes. Frances was going on seven, Georgia was five, and Eliza was nearly four years old, all too young to realize the consequences of this moment, and yet they seemed to sense things that reached beyond their years. She put her arms around them and tried to look into their eager faces to comfort them, but she couldn't meet their eyes. She bowed her head and tears came. The words she started to say choked in her throat, and she tenderly pushed the children back. She rose and went to the canvas flap that served as a door to their crude shelter and climbed up the packed snow passageway to the surface and looked out, but she saw only the white wilderness that had been her prison for so long, where only the treetops inched above the snow.

Snow. More snow piled on top of snow, layer upon layer, day after day! Tamsen could remember when she had thought such a sight was beautiful, where the trees sparkled in the winter sun and the hills were layered in white frosting. But that was when she was a girl back in Massachusetts. Now, here in the high Sierra Nevada mountains, where the deepening snows of a savage winter had blocked the passage to California and had continued relentlessly, silently, to smother them in its heavy white blanket, there was no beauty. There was only the horrible, colorless, unrelenting ghost of death, choking them, burying them.

God was surely punishing them, she thought. Why else would He have led their little caravan so close to the Promised Land, the valley of the Sacramento, only to block their passage? Their ordeal had begun in October, and now it was the end of February and into March. Or had the Devil taken over their destiny long before October? Was it back on the Nevada desert that it started, when the wagon train company had banished Jim Reed for a killing that was not a crime, but self-defense? Or was it even earlier, when they had made the mistake of taking the Hastings cut-off instead of the well-established northern route? That was a rash decision that she had argued against, but her husband had decided the matter. He had been elected leader of the party because he was a warm-hearted, likeable, easygoing old man of sixty-two, and he had the right to decide such matters even though he lacked leadership ability and the foresight necessary to deal with a crisis. Yes, she had opposed that foolish decision, and her husband had joked, "There's no opposition a man can face that's more powerful than a wiry little woman that's made up her mind." She knew all too well the guiding principle that a wife must not question, at least out loud, the judgment of her husband, so she said no more about it. Accordingly, their wagon train had turned south, down toward the Humboldt Sink, to seek a mythical pass through the jagged granite mountains that blocked their way to California.

Now they were snowbound and starving. The lead segment of the party, the large Murphy clan, had found refuge in an old trapper's cabin at the edge of the lake lying at the very base of the high mountain precipices; and there was a second small cabin nearby, which had been appropriated by the Kesebergs and others. But the Donner wagons had been forced to stop six or seven miles behind and make their own shelter at a place they called Alder

Creek. Their wagons were big, carrying a heavy load of freight to support their new life in California, and commodious enough to provide every comfort needed to ease their toilsome journey. But an axle had broken on one of the wagons, and it cost them a day's delay to repair it. The main party had left them behind, hoping to get over the mountain before the threatening storm broke over them to pin them down. Just one more day would have made the difference.

That broken axle! In trying to repair it George had cut his hand. The wound was slight, but infection had set in. Before long his whole hand was swollen and his arm began to grow numb. That had happened in October, and now it was March. The blood poisoning had turned to gangrene and it was too late even to amputate the arm; now George lay on a cot in their crude shelter with pneumonia in his lungs, and the coarse breathing in his throat foretold death.

Tamsen came back into the shack, which was now half-buried in the snow. The little girls were waiting to be told what to do. A decision had to be made. The children were strong enough to endure the journey over the mountains, for she had carefully portioned their meager scraps of food to make it last. Even the hide of their last dead animal she had boiled for soup before letting the children chew the scraps to put substance in their stomachs. She had managed her dwindling food supply so well that Tamsen and the girls were not yet the specters of skin and bones that the others had become.She was in condition to survive the ordeal of the journey and could look after her children and be for them the mother they would need as they grew up. Not for a single day during their entire lives had they ever been separated, but now if she sent them out alone, they would grow up among strangers and never know their mother.

Like the leaves of an open book flipped by the wind, her thoughts flashed back to other times and places. When did it all start? At fifteen she was already a school teacher. In her twenties she had married Mark Dozier, and they had gone west to Illinois.

She had two children, but the marriage was bad, and she had taken the babies and run away. Aunt Betsy and Tamsen had talked at length about these early years.

"Did you have a good reason for leaving Dozier?" Betsy had asked.

"As I look back on it now, maybe not," Tamsen had answered. "I was young then, and probably too selfish."

"Do you think you might have gone back to him if he hadn't died while you were away?"

"That's possible. I have often thought it might have been my fault that he died. If I had been there I might have nursed him. The neighbors talked about me, and I felt bad about it. I prayed for forgiveness, but God did not forgive me."

"Don't blame yourself," Betsy had said. "That must have been just God's will. I think there must be some big plan that works out people's lives, and there's nothing you can do about it. So don't punish yourself for something you couldn't help."

"But God saw fit to punish me," Tamsen had insisted. "It was after that that my babies both died of diphtheria. They were taken away from me for some reason, I'm sure. It was as if God was telling me that I did not deserve to have a family. Oh, how I prayed for a second chance!"

Tamsen remembered that Aunt Betsy had been a great comfort to her in those long talks about God and the great scheme of things that influenced their lives. And she remembered other things that seemed to prove some kind of pattern in her life. She had become a schoolteacher again for a time, and then in her thirties she had met George Donner. He was a widower, considerably older than Tamsen, and already had a family, two young girls, Elitha and Leanna. He needed help and Tamsen needed a home. So they were married, and she assumed the role of mother again looking after George's girls, who were in her mind God's replacement for her own two lost children. George's brother Jacob was also a widower with a family to raise, and like George he married a younger woman, Elizabeth. Now new families were started for both men.

They were prosperous farmers and had every reason to stay where they were and work their soil and grow rich, but they both caught the California fever. So in 1846 they had sold everything, equipped several large wagons for comfort during the long journey across the plains and over the mountains to the new Garden of Eden in the West.

George and Tamsen were not poor. They had sewed $10,000 in bank notes into a quilt; they would need it to buy land and livestock in the new land. And they had a box of silver dollars hidden in the tool chest of a wagon. They would get a good start in California.

Tamsen had grown to love her husband. George was a hearty, good-natured man, easy to live with. And when her first child, Frances, was born, Tamsen felt that at last God was giving her a family again. But that was then, a time when a family would find love and strength in each other in a secure place where they could plan and prepare for dangers that might lie ahead. But now, with their path blocked by a mountain of snow and their destiny hidden beyond their knowledge or control, the pattern of her life had become like a mass of snarled yarn with no clear end to be found in the tangle. The past was over, and this was now. The men were coming in from burying the body of her closest friend, Aunt Betsy. As if the Four Horsemen of the Apocalypse had dismounted and were standing before her, they loomed tall in the shadows of the crude shack, waiting.

"It's abut time," Stone said. His voice was a low whine that made her shudder. She looked at him and Cady as if pleading for help. She reached down and gently touched her husband's face, but her hand was trembling. She looked at the three little girls huddled in their corner. She took a deep breath, and then gave a long sigh of resignation.

"You can take the girls," she said slowly. "I'll stay."

Clark and Baptiste went outside, but Cady and Stone waited. They had something more to say.

"Well, now, ma'am," Stone said, "like Eddy told you, we'll take the girls out, but they're pretty small. The big'n can walk, but the two little'ns will have to be carried. We can tote 'em out, all right, but they'll get purty hefty a-fore it's over. Them's a lot of long miles to go, and there'll be whatever food you can spare to add to the weight." His voice trailed off into a kind of question.

"What are you getting at?" Tamsen demanded. She sensed a new danger here.

"Well, Missis Donner, we know that you've got money. Maybe a lot of money, And you'll never be able to get it out, even if you was to be rescued, which ain't likely. So we thought that you might want to pay us something, just to make sure that everything come off all right."

Her face tightened with a sudden flash of anger. Then she felt a cold, numbing fear that quickened her senses. Alert and tense now, with the realization that she was dealing with scoundrels, she felt her way cautiously.

"Why, it's only seven miles from here over to the lake where Mr. Eddy is. He'll see that the children are taken out," she said.

"Yes'm, but maybe we'll have to lug 'em all the way up and over." Stone was bargaining, now, and he knew he had the advantage.

"Well, I never heard of such a thing. Nobody else has charged money for saving people's lives," she parried.

"Maybe yes, maybe no. But that's neither here nor there. It's fifty miles or more that we'd have to tote them young'uns, and who knows what might happen?"

"How much do you want?" She knew she had no alternative.

"We was thinkin' that maybe five hundred dollars would be about right," Stone said, looking at Cady for confirmation. "It ain't as if you didn't have the money. You've got it, all right, and maybe a whole lot more."

"And if I give you the five hundred dollars?"

"Then you won't need to worry, ma'am. We'll take 'em. As we see it, there's no two ways about it if you want 'em out of here." Stone knew that he had won. Perhaps he should have asked for more.

"I'll pay it," she said finally. "You wait outside, and I'll get the girls ready."

The two men joined Clark and Baptiste outside, and Tamsen set about her work. She pulled out a heavy chest that was hidden in one of the wagons that formed part of the snow-covered shelter. From it she took out the money, and with it some family valuables she thought the girls should take with them—a locket, a gold ring, a brooch that her mother had given her, and a dozen silver spoons from the family set—little things to remind them of the family they once had.

A faint cry from little Sammy, Elizabeth's baby, called her back to the reality at hand. He was wrapped in blankets but was still cold. She took him up tenderly and placed him in bed with her husband with the thought that they could get warmth from each other. That done, she spoke to the little girls, who had remained silent and watchful through the whole situation. They came forward, and she put her arms around them.

"It's time for you to go," she said softly. "You are big girls now, and you can get along without your mama anymore. I must stay here with papa. He needs me. I promised I would never leave him, and I must keep my promise. You must always keep your promises, too. Do you understand?"

"Yes, mama," they answered.

"That's my big girls!" she said, with all the courage she could muster.

"But we don't want to go," Frances said. "We want to stay here with you and papa."

"No you must go. You must grow up to be fine ladies. And whenever anybody asks you who you are you must always say, 'We are the children of Mister and Missis George Donner.' Can you remember that?"

"Yes, mama."

"And you, Frances, you are the oldest and you must take care of your little sisters. You will be their mama from now on."

Frances nodded, but said nothing.

"And you must be very brave and strong going over the mountains," Tamsen went on. "And always remember to be good girls. Your papa and I expect you to be good girls. And brave." The tears came, and there was nothing more she could say.

It was time for them to dress in their warmest clothes for the ordeal. They were wearing their long underwear and woolen stockings. Their shoes were high-laced boots that she had bought for the travel, knowing that somewhere along the way they would have to walk over rough and rocky ground. Their dresses were neat and clean, and as they put them on Tamsen thought to herself, the daughters of George and Tamsen Donner must always look their best. Their caps were of knitted wool that came down over their ears and tied like bonnets under their chins. Knitted mittens were tied to a string that reached up the sleeves and around the shoulders. Frances put on her long, gray woolen coat with a high collar and big buttons down the front. The younger girls had coats that were alike, of beautiful red wool trimmed with white rabbit fur at the collar, cuffs, and down the front. They must not be like poor vagabonds, these Donner children.

For each of them Tamsen wrapped a little bundle containing four of the silver spoons and one of the pieces of family jewelry. These were tucked safely into the coat pockets. And each girl carried a little sack of food—all the dried meat left from a small bear that had been shot weeks earlier. It was the last of the food that remained in the Donner camp.

"Now I think you are ready," Tamsen said. "Remember, if anyone asks who you are, what are you going to tell them?"

"We are the children of Mister and Missis George Donner," each girl answered in turn.

"Now you must say goodbye to your father. He is sleeping, but he'll know."

Outside, the men were waiting. Tamsen gave Stone the money, and the little procession started up the faint trail marked only by deep footprints in the snow. Stone led Georgia by the hand, Cady carried Eliza on his back, and Frances followed without help. Clark and Baptiste waited with Tamsen, watching the plodding figures until they disappeared around a ridge. Then the two men went to the half-buried wagon that served as their cave.

Slowly and in silence Tamsen walked back down the sloping snow path and entered the darkening shelter. She went over to the cot where George lay and found that he had regained consciousness. He reached out and she took his hand, and darkness came.

That night little Sammy died.

At daybreak Clark and Baptiste carried the child's body out and buried it under the deep snow near Elizabeth. When they came back they found Tamsen tense and agitated.

"I'm worried," she said. "I have the girls on my mind. I did what was needful, but I can't feel right about it."

"Yes'm," Clark said. He couldn't think of anything worth saying, though he wished somehow to comfort her.

"Mister Clark," she said. "I wonder if you and Baptiste would go over to the lake and see if the children got away all right. The big storm hasn't broke yet, and they ought to be . . ." She didn't finish the words, but in her mind she saw her little ones struggling through the snow high in the cliffs that reached into the western sky.

"Yes'm, we'll do that right now." Clark felt sorry for the woman, and this was a reasonable request.

When the two had disappeared around the ridge, Tamsen busied herself tending to the needs of her husband. His hand was numb but his arm was burning with the infection and he was in great pain.

That afternoon Clark returned without Baptiste. He entered the shelter, and his face showed that something was wrong.

"Did the party get away as Mister Eddy said they would?" Tamsen asked. Clark's expression only increased her anxiety.

"Well, yes'm, they did. Captain Fallon come in with another rescue party and about twenty of 'em left this morning, them that could travel. But your girls was not among 'em."

"Oh, my God!" the mother cried under her breath. "What about Stone and Cady?"

"Well, they lit out with the rest of 'em. The way I heer'd it, somebody offered 'em some money to take their young'ns out, and so they left your girls and took somebody else."

"I was a fool." The distraught mother clenched her fists in anger.

"Well, they might get out yet, ma'am. Mister Eddy stayed behind, and Tom Miller and Mister Thompson, that come in yesterday, are still there to help him. There's a few people left that can make it, and they're all supposed to go out come daylight tomorrow."

"What happened to the girls?" She didn't care about the others; she had seen death and greed and villainy enough to harden her to the fate of anyone but her own.

"Well, the way Frances told it to me, Clark and Cady took 'em over the trail for about three miles or so, and the little'ns was gettin' pretty tired, so they stopped for a rest. And then Clark and Cady left 'em there and went off by themselves. Then they stopped, and Frances could see that they was arguin' some between theirselves, and she figured that her and her sisters was goin' to git left. But then pretty soon the fellers come back and got 'em and took 'em on over to the lake. And that's where they are now."

"Are they safe? Where are they staying? Are they with the Murphys?"

"No, there's just a few of the Murphys left, and Old Miz Murphy is about to die, so they couldn't stay there. The girls are at Keseberg's cabin."

"Keseberg's!" she screamed. The Keseberg family had gone out with an earlier party, but the guides had refused to take the man because of his inhuman conduct. He had even taken the Eddy baby before it had died, and everybody believed that he had eaten its withered flesh to sustain his own strength.

At the mention of Keseberg's name, Tamsen snatched a blanket from her cot, threw it over her head, and swept past Clark heading for the trail. George Donner moaned faintly and tried to speak, but the frantic woman did not hear.

"Mister Clark, you and Baptiste stay here with Mister Donner and do what you can for him," she ordered. She was already out of the shelter and racing to save her children from peril.

Clark shouted to her, "You don't have to worry. Keseberg ain't there now. Eddy said he would shoot him if he ever saw him, and Keseberg ain't showed himself. He's off hidin' in a cave somewhere, I reckon." But Clark couldn't tell whether she heard him or not.

At the lake she found the girls in the Keseberg cabin frightened, but safe. "Oh, my darlings," she murmured, as she clasped them in her arms. Then she lost no time in seeking out Eddy.

"I'm sorry about this Miz Donner," Eddy said. "But there was nothing I could do about it. The girls are all right, though, and I'll take 'em out with me and the last of the stragglers come daylight tomorrow morning."

"I'll pay you well, Mister Eddy," she said. "You can't leave them just to die here. I'll give you fifteen hundred dollars if you'll promise on your oath that you'll take care of them."

"No, Miz Donner, I can't do that."

"I'll get you the money." She was pleading now. "I'll go back to Alder Creek tonight and get you the money."

"No," he said flatly. "It ain't a matter of money. Besides, it would just add that much to the load. No, we'll take 'em, you can depend on that."

"God bless you, Mister Eddy," she murmured.

"We'll get away early. That storm's about to break any time, now, and I want to get as high as daylight will take us before we have to stop and maybe sit out the storm."

"You're a good man, Mister Eddy," was all she could say.

"I think you ought to reconsider, ma'am, and come along with us," he advised,and she knew there was wisdom in his words.

"No, I must do what's needful here," she responded slowly and went back to her children for their last night together.

When the heavy, gray morning came and the little party was preparing to depart, Clark and Baptiste appeared. They had abandoned the helpless Donner at Alder Creek and now stood awkwardly before her. She knew that they both wanted to leave with the rest. To stay behind could mean certain death for them, for there was to be no further rescue from the lake.

"You must go along, both of you," she said. "There is nothing more you can do here. I'll feel better with you helping to look after the girls."

They nodded and eagerly joined the group. The boy Baptiste, who had been so loyal to the Donners all the way, left her with the momentary hesitation of a bird suddenly released from its cage making up its mind which way to fly to join others of its kind in freedom.

She stood alone in the snow and watched the little party start its long journey to the uncertain promise of a new life. William Foster took charge of Simon Murphy, his wife's little brother; a man named Thompson was leading Frances Donner by the hand; William Eddy and Hiram Miller hoisted her two precious bundles, Georgia and Eliza, on their shoulders so the girls could ride piggyback, each with a blanket made into a sling that tied over the forehead of the strong men who carried them. A few others trudged along the trail made by the leaders, and the stillness of desolation settled over the place. Only Keseberg remained, hiding somewhere among the trees, perhaps watching this last movement of life.

Tamsen saw the little group climb a ridge beyond the lake. Then, before they had disappeared from sight, she turned and faced the trail leading back to Alder Creek. Without looking back, she plodded along the tracks she had made the night before. The threatening storm swept down upon her with relentless fury. Blown by the wind, the slanting sleet stung her face, and she pulled the blanket closer over her head and shoulders.

As she neared her squalid shelter, the wind slackened and the sleet turned to snow. The big white flakes floated gently, silently down, and snow filled the tracks she left behind her.

Remme's Ride

THE DAY WAS beginning well for Jules Remme. In a restaurant in Sacramento he had just finished a good breakfast and was ready to enjoy an expensive cigar. He had sold his herd and had in his pocket a bank draft for $12,500. At last, after years of hard work and careful dealing he could now say he had the means for a secure and comfortable future. He leaned back, blew a puff of smoke,and reached for the morning newspaper.

The headline that met his eye was cold and shocking: ADAMS BANKS FAIL! Reading on, he learned that there had been a financial crash back in St. Louis and some of the banks there had closed their doors. This had brought about a chain reaction that caused the Adams Express Company Bank to close in San Francisco. One must assume, therefore, that the branch banks of the Adams Company would also close, including the one in Sacramento. For Remme the news could not have been worse. The draft he had in his pocket, which meant his entire fortune, was to be drawn on the Adams Banks.

Remme was a cattleman and a stock buyer. In 1855 a stockman in California could do well, buying from the small ranchers and selling to the markets in the cities like San Francisco and Sacramento. Such transactions required an outlay of cash for purchases, and by the time an accumulated herd was sold the amount of the investment could be considerable. Remme had sold his cattle and deposited his money in the Adams bank just a few days earlier. Now all he had was a little piece of paper, a certificate of deposit, which would be worthless unless he could get to an Adams Bank and withdraw his money.

He grabbed his hat, dashed out of the restaurant, and hurried over to the bank. As he feared, there was a long line of people clamoring to get in, but the doors were closed. A sign in the window said that the bank would not open. Depositors might later be paid a small fraction of their claims, but there was no guarantee that they would get anything.

Remme ran back to his hotel and looked at the newspaper article again. The news had come from San Francisco, so he knew the bank there would have been the first to close. As he was considering what to do next, a friend of his walked into the lobby.

"You've heard the news about the Adams Bank, I guess?" Remme asked.

"Yes, I heard last night." The friend worked for a steamship company that operated boats running from San Francisco to Sacramento and then on up the Sacramento River to Colusa. If anyone could know what was going on, he would be the one.

"Well," said Remme, "I'm a stuck pig. All my money, twelve thousand five hundred dollars, is in the Adams banks. How am I goin' to get it out? Do you think I could get to the Marysville or Placerville branch before they get the word?"

"No, that ain't likely. The letters to them surely came up river yesterday along with the notice to the Sacramento branch. They'll be closed today, too. No use thinking in that direction."

"There must be other branches further away that wouldn't have got the word yet. What about Grass Valley?" Remme was desperate. If he could outrun the message, perhaps he could cash his draft and recover his life's savings.

"The only one I can think of that might not have the orders yet would be the one in Portland. It would take some time for a letter to get up the coast to them, but that wouldn't do you any good. You couldn't get to Portland in time."

"There are no stage lines all the way to Portland. How do you think the news will get to them?"

"By steamboat, surely." The friend seemed to know what he was talking about. "As a matter of fact, there's a ship scheduled to leave San Francisco for Portland tomorrow morning. It's the *Columbia,* and I'd bet a dollar to a doughnut that she'll be carrying the order, and possibly with a messenger on board, to the Portland bank."

"Maybe I could make it on horseback and beat the ship."

"You're crazy, man. It's at least seven hundred miles from here to Portland, more or less, and some of it just freight roads and pack trails."

"But I can't lose that money. It's not just my money, anyway. I borrowed the capital to get started from my father back in Illinois, and he can't afford to lose it. If I'm wiped out he's wiped out, too, and a whole life's savings would be gone up in smoke. I'd take a go at it even if it killed me. If I could get fresh horses along the way, and if I could ride night and day, do you think I could beat that ship? How long do you think it'll take the ship to reach Portland?"

"I'd say five, six days, maybe a week."

"Well, I just can't sit here. I've got to try."

"One thing I can tell you that might help a little," the friend said. "I've got to admire your spirit, even if you are out of your head. What I can tell you—and this is confidential information—is that the *Columbia* will be taking a company of soldiers—no, two companies of soldiers—that will have to be unloaded with all their equipment at Humboldt Bay and at the mouth of the Rogue River. That will delay the ship considerably. With good luck you might beat the ship, but it'll be nip and tuck."

In Remme's mind the question of whether the *Columbia* would carry the message to close the Adams Bank in Portland was settled. That would be a certainty. The real problem that remained was to get there first. The news of the ship's delay, therefore, was the encouragement he needed. The odds would be on his side, but only if he had the stamina for the long ride, if he could get fresh horses along the way, if there were no accidents or miscalculations, if the ship took a little extra time to unload the soldiers, if a snowstorm did not bury him in the high Trinity Mountains that he would have to cross. And if—but Remme could not allow himself to think of such possibilities now; he could only think of winning.

"One thing more," the friend volunteered. He was beginning to sense the drama of the situation, and he thought of the old saying that God looks after fools and the world admires a man who can bet his whole pile and even his life on a single play of the game. "If it'll help you any, my company has a river boat that will be leaving the Sacramento docks in about an hour going up river. I can get you on that and it'll take you far enough to give you a good start."

"I'll take it!" exclaimed Remme. Action was what he needed most at that moment. So when the river boat left Sacramento at noon, Remme was on it. He paced the deck and inwardly raged at the slow progress the steamer made as it chugged up river, edging around the tree-lined bends and creeping past the many small landings where farmers whose acres bordered the river had erected makeshift docks for unloading freight or loading produce.

For an impatient man this was agony. By the time the boat reached Knight's Landing, Remme had had enough. He got off and headed for the little adobe shack where Mr. Knight was supposed to be. He had met the old man a time or two before and knew him to be fair in his dealings and wise in the ways of the frontier. Knight had prospected for gold but had found very little. Disillusioned, he had turned to ranching, but he had no talent or taste for such work, and finally he had settled on the river where his landing became a popular center for the distribution of goods from the freight boats to the ranches and villages in the valley. And by now, Knight had become a temperamental, cynical, irascible old codger with an excessive taste for rum.

Fortunately for Remme, Knight was reasonably sober and in a good mood that day. In the manner of the West, little time was wasted on small talk. While Remme explained his predicament and his plan to solve the problem, the old man lit his pipe and looked at the ceiling. Then he shook his head.

"You're a spry young feller, I'll say that for you, and you've got grit, but nobody can ride from here to Portland a-horseback and beat that steamer out there on the ocean."

"I aim to try, even if it kills me."

"It probably will. Anyhow, you'd need mighty good horse flesh for that ride. How you gonna manage that?"

"Well, I thought I could get a horse and saddle from you to start with, and then I could trade off along the way."

"You might trade horses often enough, all right, but you'd need money to boot. You got any money?"

"Yes, a couple of hundred dollars in my pocket, and that's all."

"Even then, you might get took up for horse stealin'," Knight said. "Here, take a drink and think it over some more. It ain't too late to change your mind."

"I was bettin' on you to start me out," Remme insisted.

"Well, if you're so dad blamed set on it, yes, I could let you have a horse and saddle."

The deal was made, and Remme headed north along the road that followed the river. The horse was in good shape, the gallop was steady, and Remme felt comfortable in the rhythm of the gait. At sunset he was passing the Sutter Buttes, a ruggedly beautiful landmark in the Sacramento Valley. The wagon road he was following stayed near the river, and its many sharp bends and wide sweeping curves began to worry Remme. He was wasting precious time tracing the extra miles along the river road when he could just as easily cut straight toward Red Bluff on trails that connected the scattered ranches along the western slopes of the valley.

There was another reason for taking the short cut. Not many miles away and almost directly in his path was the ranch owned and operated by the Widow Elkins, and Remme was beginning to feel hunger. He hadn't eaten since morning, and he knew that a good supper could be had for the asking at the Elkins place. He had bought some cattle from her the year before and remembered her as a hearty woman, generous and affable. Twilight was fading into dusk as he rode into the Elkins yard.

"Well, as I live and breathe!" exclaimed the woman as soon as she saw him. "If it ain't Jules Remme! What brings you here?"

"Hello, Jenny. Just passin' through, and I had a notion that I could get a bite to eat from you, and maybe some grain and water for my horse."

"You're shore welcome. You just put your horse in the shed and feed him, and come in the house. I'll fix up something for you, and right glad to do it."

Remme had remembered her as a good looking woman, and now as he sat at her kitchen table watching her prepare the meal in the light of the tallow candles, he began to sense a deeper beauty in the woman. She was what you might call buxom, with pleasantly found features and dark hair that was wound into a knot held by combs on top of her head. Her body movements were graceful as she worked fast and efficiently at the kitchen stove.

"I'm in kind of a hurry," he said, and as she worked he explained his problem to her. She listened in silence, and when he had finished his story she went to the cupboard and brought out a jug of whiskey and poured him a generous drink.

"Here, you'll need this," she said. "And I think I'll have one with you. I don't touch this stuff very often, but this is an occasion." She seemed to be weighing her words carefully. "As you know, I run this place alone, ever since Jed died, with no help around but the Indians. It ain't often that a real man comes along that's more than half way civilized, and here you are, a sight for sore eyes." She put the food before him and sat down to watch him eat. "I've already et, but you just take right a-hold." She was studying him with deep interest.

Jules Remme was what might be considered a handsome man, tall and wiry-slender, with broad shoulders and the swell of muscles under the sleeves and chest of his jacket. His face was tan, as a man's should be under the California sun, and his brownish eyes suggested both an alert intelligence and a depth of passion that a woman might read as real character. The broad mustache was shaped in the popular style of the time, drooping at the edges, and his square chin indicated strength and determination. A woman could like him. Jenny Elkins sat across the table from him, and as he ate she studied her drink, slowly tracing the rim of the glass with one finger. "There's no way you're goin' to beat that ship to the Oregon Territory," she said.

"I've got to try. If I don't make it, I stand to lose everything I have in the world."

"There's more to life than just money," she said. "You could start over. And anyway, if you think you can win that race, you're just dreaming."

"Every man's got to have a dream, Jenny."

"Maybe so," she admitted. But she was a woman who had learned to face reality. "But the fact is," she said, changing the subject, "it's fixin' to rain. Winter ain't over yet, and you know what a heavy rain can be like in the valley, and there'll be mountains to cross with some pretty deep snow, and maybe storms all the way."

"I know," he said. "But I'll make it."

She had to admire his determination. A woman, without trying too hard, could be happy with such a man, she thought.

He rose and made ready to leave. "I'm much obliged," was all he said. She rose and stood close to him and her eyes, intensely serious, looked into his.

"Well, then," she said slowly, "why don't you get some rest first? If you're of a mind to, you can stay here tonight and get a fresh start early in the morning."

"I can't do that, Jenny. You know that as well as I do," he said, backing out the door. "I've got this rope around my horns and it's pulling on me. Under other circumstances—"

"I know," she said. He led the horse to the front porch and was ready to mount when she came out with a small bundle in her arms. "That rain'll soak you to the bone," she said. "So here's an oilskin coat that used to be Jed's. It'll help some. And here's some bread and meat. You'll be missin' a few meals along the way."

"God bless you, Jenny. I'll remember this."

As he lifted his foot to the stirrup, she gently put her hand on his arm. "Good luck," was all she said. He quickly mounted and rode on his way.

It was about ten o'clock when he reached the village of Red Bluff. The rain had started, and he was grateful for the topcoat that Jenny Elkins had given him. At the livery stable he was able to make a horse trade and without further delay was on the road again. Another twenty miles, and he was nearing the upper end of the Sacramento Valley. When he went through Shasta City the town was sleeping. At Whiskytown only a barking dog or two sensed his passing. Remme was tired and sleepy, but he pushed on.

At the Tower House, a roadside inn near French Gulch, he left the road, which would have taken him westward to Weaverville and down along the Trinity River to Humboldt Bay. He had been climbing steadily, and from here on he would have to follow the steep trail used by pack mule teams bringing freight and supplies from the coast over the Trinity Alps to the little mining camps at Sawyer's Bar and Coffee Creek in the valleys to the north. The rain had turned to sleet and snow, and the trail was difficult to follow, particularly in the dark. The coming of dawn made little difference in the blinding snow. When daylight came he realized that he had lost the trail.

He found himself in a box canyon that led to nowhere. To make matters worse, he seemed to have lost his sense of direction. He could turn around and get out of the canyon, but from there he would still be lost. The rain and slush had obliterated what faint tracks he might have left. He was supposed to be bearing northward, but now he was not sure which direction was north. The dark, cloudy sky hid the sun, and he felt that any way he turned could be north.

Back out of the tight canyon, he found himself in a broad valley. He reasoned that the pack trail would probably cross the valley at some point, so he decided to ride in a wide circle; somewhere he would surely pick up the trail. He was tired and miserable, and the loss of time added to his discomfort. But more important was the need to keep his head. To be lost in the mountains during a storm could bring panic, and he knew that many a person in such circumstances and lacking the mountaineer's instincts and experience had perished. I must keep my head, he thought, but the heavy chill of fear was beginning to smother his senses.

When he did find what looked like the faint outline of a trail his relief was only momentary; another problem faced him. He had come upon it at an exact right angle. Being turned around in his sense of direction, he had no way of knowing whether to follow it to the right or the left. To make the wrong choice would bring him back to the Tower House, and time would be lost. Yet he had no feeling for either the right or the left. Like a machine stuck at dead center, he couldn't choose either way. The horse stood still, with his head down, waiting for a decision that Remme could not make. Then he remembered that animals were supposed to have instincts that would lead them home from great distances through unknown country. "Horse," he said,"I guess you'll have to make the decision; I sure as hell can't."

He gave the horse free reign and gently kicked his side. The horse slowly stepped forward and turned left. The animal had given him his clue. He turned the horse around and headed in the opposite direction. The horse had started toward home. Therefore the trail that would take Remme on up into the mountains and over to the mining camps beyond would have to lead the other way. Valuable time had been lost, and the steamer *Columbia* would be somewhere between San Francisco and Humboldt Bay. The race was on.

The Trinity Alps were rugged, and the trail in places was steep. His horse slowed to a walk and at times had to strain hard to get over the ledges and around huge boulders. Rain and snow had made the rocky trail slippery; in some places it was dangerously narrow, a mere strip between steep cliffs above and a perpendicular drop below. Going down the other side was just as precarious. This wild country was new to him, but he had heard stories of how whole pack trains, drivers and all, had slipped and plunged to their death on the rocks below.

After many slow hours he reached Sawyer's Bar only to find the camp deserted. In winter such remote places closed down; the miners could not get supplies and the weather made placer mining impossible. This was late February, and life would not come back to the camp for at least another month. Remme followed the trail on to Fort Jones, which was a little nearer to civilization. There he managed to get a welcome cup of coffee and some food, but no fresh horse was to be had. His poor animal, now almost dead from fatigue, would have to take him on to Yreka.

The storm had let up by the time he reached Yreka, but there was little comfort in his relief. He was told that there was no livery stable in town. "People around here own their own horses," he was told. "The only one in this town that might have an extra horse or two would be Elisha Steele. He runs cattle and he's friendly to the Indians around here, so he might break down and part with a horse."

But at the Steele place Remme did not get a warm welcome.

"I ain't lookin' for no horse trade," Steele said. "And even if I was, that critter of yours is all tuckered out. You've used him up bad. I wouldn't take him as a gift."

"Well, then, could I buy one from you?"

"Nope. You just better settle down till this sorry bag of coyote bait can take you to where you want to go, if you have any place in particular to get to." Remme was desperate. The steamboat would surely have reached Humboldt Bay by now, and time could not be wasted. Tired as he was in body, his mind came alive.

"Well, you see, it's this way. I've just come over the Trinities, and I'm chasing some horse thieves. They got away with six good mares from the Ide ranch in Red Bluff, and I think they're headin' for the Oregon Territory, and I've been gaining on 'em. I'm a U.S. Marshal, and I've got papers to prove it, and if those horse thieves get away a lot more people than me will be sorry."

"Horse thieves, you say." Remme could see that his lie was

beginning to work. "Horse thieves is different. They should always get caught and punished good and proper. I guess a body ought to do what he can to help catch such scum of the earth."

The morality of the West dictated that such criminals should be caught at any price and promptly hanged without argument. Elisha Steele, cattleman and friend of the Indians—who were frequently falsely accused of such depravities—believed in this code of honor.

"Maybe I could let you have a horse, then. I can't allow you much on this poor beast, but I guess if you're a marshal you'll get paid back for the price of a horse. I've got a good one here. Them Siskiyou Mountains are pretty rough this time of year, but once you get on the other side you'll have them horse thieves by the tail with a downhill pull. And by the way, you better keep a sharp eye out for Indians. Some Klamath renegades are on the war path, and they'll get you if you let 'em."

With a fast horse under him once again, Remme headed for the high range that marked the border between California and Oregon. His legs ached, his back ached, his head ached, and he was sleepy, but a least he was on his way and the race was still on. The mountains were not as rugged and treacherous as the Trinities, but they were higher. The winter snows still capped the peaks and lay packed deep in the canyons. The trail had been traveled recently, so it was easy to follow, but the skies were ominously black. A storm was coming, and he sensed that it would be a bad one.

First came the rain, a cold driving rain from the west. As he climbed higher and higher into the mountains the slanting rain became sleet and snow. He was glad to have the oilskin coat that Jenny Elkins had given him, but the stinging cold sleet burned his face. Jenny Elkins. Her warm kitchen was both a memory and a pleasant fantasy now. It was night again, and he feared that he could get lost in the storm. The poor horse, still climbing, had slowed to a walk. Remme knew it would be futile to go on; he would have to find shelter of some kind and pass the night as best he could. Near the trail he found a large stump of a dead tree. Limbs and brush had sheltered it on one side from the storm and it was still dry enough, he thought, to burn. In the cold, wet air, even the dry tinder refused to ignite immediately, but after repeated tries he managed to get a fire going. To his great relief the stump began to burn on the dry side.

With numb fingers he tied his horse to a large fir tree nearby, which provided a meager shelter against the storm, and the wretched beast stood with head down, humped against the cold. Remme crouched close to his fire and warmed his hands. His buckskin gloves were wet, and he placed them not too close to the fire to dry out a little.

The burning stump radiated its warmth, like its light, only a few feet into the cold, drenching darkness. Remme huddled by the fire; his face and hands were warm, too hot for comfort, while has back was freezing. When he turned his back to the fire, the penetrating cold once again numbed his face, hands, and chest. Like a beef roasting on a spit, he turned and turned, with one side scorching and the other side always freezing. Only brief snatches of sleep were possible.

The hours passed. By morning the sleet had turned to snow, which fell thick and heavy over trees and rocks and trail. Under the oilskin coat he had been able to keep his precious bank draft dry, and also what was left of the bread and meat that Jenny Elkins had so thoughtfully given him. He ate the remainder of his food, gave his horse a handful of grain from his saddle bag, and watched the thick blanket of snow grow silently deeper and more forbidding. It was time to move on.

Down the north slopes of the mountains the way became easier. He hoped to make it across the Rogue River before he had to change horses again. The steamboat *Columbia* had surely reached Humboldt Bay and by now had probably discharged its load of soldiers, so he knew he could not stop for the rest he so badly needed. But at least he was making progress.

As he neared Rogue River a new problem suddenly came upon him. He had left the snowstorm behind and the trail was clearly visible once again, but as he rode through a cluster of trees near the river he heard the zing of a bullet pass near his head. A second later he heard the shot, which came from somewhere on his right. He had forgotten the warning of Elisha Steele that the Klamath Indians were killing whites in the territory. He kicked his horse to full speed and crouched low to make less of a target. Two more shots whizzed over his head. This time the reports came from behind him. At least, he was outrunning his attackers, who were probably, he reasoned, a small band of renegades from the Klamath reservation. He heard one more shot, now fainter and far behind, and he began to feel safe again.

At the scrubby little settlement of Round Prairie (which in later years was to grow up, become prosperous, and change its name to Roseburg) he was unable to find a fresh horse, but Eugene was only a few miles ahead. There he rested a little, got a fresh horse, and resumed his journey. The new horse cost him seventy dollars, but he was able to get sixty-five dollars for the one that had carried him over the Siskiyous and had saved him from the Indians. He felt a little better about his big gamble; the cards were beginning to fall in his favor.

Mile after mile he rode, on into the long Willamette Valley. He was so tired now, he was losing track of time. Several times he fell asleep in the saddle, and when he awoke he would find the horse had slowed to a walk. Back in the galloping gait he had to think hard to keep from being drawn into the hypnotic spell of the rhythmic hoofbeats of the horse. Plickety-plock, plickety-plock, plickety-plock! Beat-the-clock! Beat-the-clock! Beat-the-clock! The monotony of the sound pulled at his sanity, and he had to think of other things. There was no order of time or place in his thoughts— the burning stump, the homing instinct of a horse, the good meal that Jenny Elkins had carried, smiling, from her stove to the table to set before him, the bank draft in his pocket, the shots of the Indians—these were all flashes of light in his head picturing recent events. His life as a cattle buyer, the many herds he had driven to market, the people he had known and those he had loved—these were images that floated in like dreams from a life lost somewhere in the past.

He thought of other dreams he had had, some that had repeated themselves again and again with the same plot but different characters; yet the crises were always the same. He would be driving a buggy to a place he had urgently to reach, but big rocks would roll in the way, or the road would turn back upon itself, or his team would run away and leave him standing at the edge of an impassable cliff. Or he had dreamed that he was making his most important sale, only to have his whole herd disappear or turn into sheep or chickens. Sometimes he had dreamed that he was falling from a high bridge, but he always woke before he crashed below. And sometimes he had dreamed of a beautiful lady, one he had never known, and she would caress him; then she would disappear or the scene would shift to something else, and he would suddenly be a preacher in church with the congregation waiting for his inspiring words, but he had lost or forgotten his sermon. He wondered whether this lifetime of frustrating dreams might be some supernatural warning of the outcome of this last adventure which was itself only a dream.

It was evening when he reached Portland. He put his horse in a livery stable, and with saddle bags over his shoulder he staggered toward a hotel near by. Walking was difficult. His leg muscles would not work, his backbone would not bend, and his head ached. He had been on the road six days with very little sleep. How many horses he had bought and sold he could not remember. When the aging night clerk at the hotel pushed the guest book toward him, he could scarcely hold the pen. The signature was an unrecognizable scrawl. But there was yet something to attend to, something he had rehearsed in his mind a hundred times.

"Will you be here on duty all night?" he asked the old man behind the desk.

"Yes. Till eight o'clock, that is."

"Well, there'll be five dollars in it for you if you'll wake me at seven o'clock. Come in and make sure I'm awake, even if I fight you. And not one minute after seven."

"Yes, sir. You can depend on it."

Remme was asleep the minute he touched the bed. And a minute later, so it seemed, the old man was waking him. He rose, still tired but in control of his thoughts once again. After shaving and cleaning up as best he could, he went down to the hotel dining room and ordered breakfast. It was a quarter to eight. The ancient night clerk hobbled in to collect his five dollars, which he proudly proclaimed as being the most generous gratuity he had ever received.

"Would you know whether the steamboat from San Francisco is in yet?" Remme asked. The hotel was not far from the river docks.

"Yep. She come in last night. I thought maybe you had come in on 'er."

Remme hurried down to the boat dock. Men were unloading cargo from the *Columbia,* piling crates on the freight platform.

"Have they taken off the mail yet?" he asked one of the workmen.

"Oh, yes. The mail always goes up first." It was now eight-thirty. The banks usually opened at nine. Remme inquired the way to the Adams Bank, and by nine o'clock he was waiting across the street. First came a corpulent man wearing a derby hat and a long top coat; he unlocked the front door and disappeared inside. This, Remme thought, would be the bank manager or head cashier. Next came two lesser personages, who were let in without ceremony. At nine-fifteen the curtains on the windows were lifted, and the door was opened. Three or four people who had been waiting entered to transact their business.

I mustn't be the first, thought Remme. Must make everything seem very routine and natural. With such a large draft to cash, I must do nothing that might arouse suspicion. He waited another ten minutes, fingering the slip of paper in his pocket.

Inside the bank he casually approached the cashier's window. The man was of middle age, he noticed, thin and weaselish in appearance. He had on the usual black double sleeves that reached almost to the elbows, and wore a visor over his forehead. A second teller had a customer at his cage, so Remme approached weaselface.

"I'd like to cash this draft," he said, pushing the note, now somewhat crumpled from its hazardous journey, through the window. The man studied it for a moment and then gave Remme a searching look.

"Twelve thousand five hundred," he said. "That's a lot of money. You say you want to cash it?"

"Yes."

"I suppose you can prove that you are who you say you are." He looked at the draft again. "Remme. Mr. Jules Remme."

Letters and other papers establishing his identify were produced, and the cautious cashier studied him intently. "I can't handle anything in this amount," he said finally. Remme's heart froze. Apparently the mail had not yet reached the bank, but here was another possible complication.

"Mr. Babcock will have to approve a transaction of this size," said the cashier. "Please come with me, Mr. Remme."

They went into a back room, where the paunchy man sat. Introductions were made, and the bank manager began to study the papers. "So you're a cattle buyer," he said. "Don't see many of your kind around here."

"Well, sir, I just came in on the *Columbia* from San Francisco, and I plan to go on up the river to the cattle country to the east of here. That's why I need the cash." Immediately Remme was sorry for his falsehood. The banker rose and went to the door, calling to a young man who was sweeping the floor.

"Hey, Joe, you go down to the post office and get the mail. The boat's in from San Francisco."

Returning to the business at hand the banker asked, "How do you want it? Bank notes?"

"No, I'd rather have it in gold if possible."

The banker went to his safe and brought out several sacks of gold coins. Slowly he began to count out the money. About half way through the operation, the door opened and Joe entered with a packet of letters which he placed on the banker's desk. Absorbed in his counting, the big man pushed the mail aside and went on with his work.

"By the way," the banker said. "You understand that in handling this amount of gold we'll have to charge you the usual rate, one-half of one percent."

Remme allowed as how that would be all right, and the banker was happy at the thought of making $62.50 on the transaction. The ten stacks of gold coins, which Remme quickly scooped into two sacks were heavy. They must weigh about forty pounds, he thought, as he lugged them to the door. The young man with the broom was outside sweeping dirt from the boards of the sidewalk, and Remme got an impish idea.

"Say, Joe," he said. "Do you have any of your own money deposited in this bank?" When Joe admitted that, yes, he did have a little of his savings there, Remme whispered, "Well, I'd advise you to go in and withdraw it immediately. This bank is about to close." And grinning all the way, he went back to his hotel.

Having assured himself that his money would be temporarily safe, he went to the livery stable and sold his horse and saddle. Then he arranged for passage on the *Columbia* back to San Francisco on its return trip starting that afternoon. He was looking forward to sleeping all the way home.

About an hour later he went back to the bank. Sure enough, the door was locked, the curtains drawn, and a sign in the window warned depositors of their impending losses.

The Bodega War

By God, I'll do it! It's time those low-down squatters were taught a lesson, and come hell or high water I've got to do it." The fact that Tyler Curtis was talking to himself made no difference; he had at last reached a decision, and to punctuate his determination he slapped his thigh so hard the horse he was riding jumped to attention expecting spur and whip. The master was a man to be obeyed.

Curtis was a tall, thin veteran of the Mexican War, a seasoned westerner made of steel and rawhide. His head was bald on top with a fringe that was beginning to turn gray at the temples, and perhaps in compensation for this vanishing adornment he wore a heavy mustache curved down at the sides of his mouth after the fashion popular in the 1850's. His cold gray eyes bespoke a strong will and a tenacity that would tolerate no opposition from lesser beings who might try to stand in his way. He was the kind of man best suited to conquer the savage West in those days when to survive took courage and to prosper required an alert mind and an uncompromising will. In short, he was the kind of man who usually got what he wanted.

"What I want most," he said to his wife later that night at supper, "is to get them damn squatters off our land. It's clear by

now that the sheriff won't help us, and we'll have to take the law
into our own hands."

Marietta agreed with him as she always did, right or wrong. In
this case, however, she shared his dream and approved his
determination.

"What I see for us," Curtis went on, "is this big ranch with cattle
and sheep on the grasslands and good timber in the hills. It's our
property, signed, sealed, and delivered, and if those farmers won't
pay their rent we'll have to put 'em out ourselves, and that's the
long and the short of it."

The property in question was a vast acreage that had been a
Spanish land grant reaching from Bodega Bay inland to the east
and southward almost to the town of Petaluma. Originally it had
been a generous gift of more than four thousand acres obtained
from the Mexican government by Captain Stephen Smith, who had
anchored his ship in the bay called Bodega on the California coast
and liked what he saw—rolling hills covered with gigantic redwood
trees, and wide valleys lush with tall grass which in winter and
spring would ripple and sway, thick and green, when the cool
breezes blew in from the west. And through the warm summer
months the color would change to a soft golden brown dotted by
clusters of green oaks. But Smith was a seaman, not a rancher. He
leased the timberland to a sawmill company to cut and mill the
redwood lumber for the building of San Francisco, and much of the
farmland he rented to settlers who had come west to take root in
California; so within two or three years little squares of farmsteads
were beginning to alter the natural pattern, each having its cabin or
shack amid the usual cluster of corrals and sheds, clear evidence that
the settlers were converting the resources of nature to their own
uses.

Smith married and built a home in a little valley a few miles
inland from the coast at a place he called Bodega Corners. The
agricultural tracts were divided into quarter sections, and Captain
Smith had allowed farmers and ranchers to move in. With some he
had arranged for annual payments of rent based on the value of the

crop or livestock produced. With others there had been no formal agreement, but Smith had not challenged their right to stay and build their homes. He had remained on friendly terms with his new neighbors because he saw in them the possibility of developing a town. A mile or so away from Smith's house, George Robinson had opened a saloon, and that was where the village began. Later, he and a fellow named Bowman opened a hotel near by, and Donald McDonald set up a store. Smith himself ran the post office, and Bodega Corners became a town.

But late in 1854 Captain Smith died, leaving his property to his widow and children. For three years nothing much happened to disturb the tranquility or growth of the community, but after Smith's death most of the farmers forgot to pay their rent, and with no one to say otherwise they began to think of the land as their own. In 1858 the Widow Smith married Tyler Curtis, and he immediately set about to put the affairs of the ranch in order. He secured legal custody of the minor children and became executor of their estate. He had the courts review and confirm the legality of Smith's claim to the land and secured writs for the eviction of the squatters. By this time there were more than a hundred families living on the vast Smith domain, and Curtis wanted them either to pay up or get out.

The law was on his side, but the county officials who had the unpleasant task of evicting so many people were in no hurry to antagonize all those voters. The stubborn settlers refused to move, and the law was slow; the sheriff never could seem to find the time to take the necessary action.

"We can't wait any longer," Curtis told his wife. "That fat no-good sheriff may look like a tub of guts, but when it comes to enforcing our rights he has no guts or backbone at all. It's clear that we've got to take matters into our own hands. It's our land, not theirs, and we have every right to sell it or use it as we see fit. The longer we let things slide the harder it will be to make them pay up or get out."

"That's right, or course," Marietta agreed. "But it looks to me like they'll fight back. So how are you going to do it?"

"You can bet they will try to fight back. We'll just have to meet force with force, and I've got a plan for that."

That same evening down at Bodega Corners a group of farmers had assembled at Robinson's saloon to quicken their spirits with a bite of "the creature" and be inspired by the impassioned words of Michael Terry, their obvious leader and spokesman. He was a giant of a man, heavy with muscles and tightly padded in the belly, the kind of fellow one might expect to see fighting or wrestling for a prize at the county fair, confident but not a bully, cold, calculating, and deliberate when facing an opponent but gentle with children and meek in the presence of ladies. But he was not as simple as he looked. What always surprised strangers and delighted his friends was a contradiction in his character that made him seem like two different persons; instead of being the sluggish bumpkin that his physical appearance suggested, he had a quick mind, a sharp wit, and a gift of speech that won him the respect of his neighbors. When Terry spoke, people listened.

"You're all good men here," he was saying. "You've been workin' your tails off just to be makin' a livin', and me too, toilin' like mules and sharin' our troubles like brothers on God's own sweet land here, and we deserve—and our wives and children, too—we've earned the right to have clothes on our backs and food in our bellies. And I'll drink to that." He raised his glass, and the men in the saloon drank with him.

"Every one of us got the same notice from that money-grubbin', flint-hearted devil of a Curtis—to pay or get out. Maybe some of you paid and some didn't. That don't matter. We're all in the same boat and headin' for a showdown sooner or later. I say we don't owe him a blessed cent, not a God-given penny from the sweat of our brow either for rent or purchase." The assembled audience murmured their agreement. "Now, here's the way I see it," he went on. "In the first place this was God's own land, and He let the Indians live on it for takin' care of it and doin' it no harm. Then the

Mexicans, that had no right to it, stole it from the Indians and said it was theirs, and then they gave it to Captain Smith—God rest his soul. And he gave it to us—him that never had to pay a cent for it in the first place—and we are the ones that have took care of it. And now comes the schemin' devil of a Curtis, him that married the forlorn widow Smith and got his hands on it that way according to the law. He never put a dollar into it, nor a drop of sweat, either, and now he wants to do us out of it and turn us out of house and home. I say it's for us to stand our ground."

"But he's got the law on his side," someone said.

"Has he, now! There's little help the law wants to give him, what with us electing the sheriff and the county attorney, what with the vote coming up again this fall. They know which side their bread is buttered on."

"That may be," another farmer said, taking a drink to solemnize his thought, "but if I know Curtis there's bound to be a fight, and somebody's bound to get hurt, maybe killed."

"If it's a fight he wants, it's a fight we'll give him!" Terry roared. "And if it's killin' he wants, it's a killin' he'll get. There's enough of us to take him, and no blame on anybody. Are you with me, boys?" The boys were with him, and the saloon vibrated with their unanimous chorus of determination to resist to the death any ruthless attempt to force them out of their homes.

Tyler Curtis, as the farmers had concluded, was less interested in collecting overdue rents than he was in gaining possession of the lands that were legally his, and as he had told his wife he had a plan. He went to San Francisco, and down at the waterfront he lost no time in recruiting a small army of men, mostly derelicts hungry for the daily wage he promised them and eager for adventure, disillusioned miners who had gone broke in the gold country, sailors who had jumped ship and were ready for any opportunity that came their way, ex-convicts from Australia, and a few left over from better days in the army. He selected a leader who seemed capable of commanding this motley force and briefly outlined his plan. Tomorrow they were to assemble with whatever arms they could find—rifles, pistols, and knives—and take passage on a ferry that would take them across the bay and up the river to Petaluma, where they would disembark and continue on foot to the Curtis place some twenty miles away. Their job was to form squads of five or six men who would pay a visit to each farmer or rancher on his property. If the settler could show evidence that he had paid his rent for the year, he was within the law and was to be passed over, but if he should prove delinquent he was to be evicted by force if necessary.

"I don't want any unprovoked violence," Curtis told them, "and I don't want anybody to get hurt if that can be avoided. I'm counting on most of them to go peaceably, but there may be a few that will put up a fight. If so, you'll know what to do, and the law will be on your side. You'll be like a posse or army, and Tom McBean, here, will be your captain." McBean had been a soldier in the Mexican war, and Curtis knew him slightly. He would be as reliable as one could expect and should be able to handle the men.

"Now remember, boys, tomorrow you'll meet at the ferry, and you'll be in Petaluma about noon; then you'll have to march on the freight road on up to my place. You should be there by next morning. I'm doing this at night because I don't want anyone to know you are coming, so don't tell anyone what you are up to; the less known the better. At my house you'll get further orders, and your pay will be waiting for you." Curtis had thus set his plan in motion, and he returned to his headquarters at Bodega.

According to schedule the little raggle-taggle army of about twenty adventurers assembled with their assorted weapons and knapsacks containing food and liquid necessities. It was afternoon when they reached Petaluma and already the men were becoming a little bored. Ahead of them lay a long, tiring march, and already a chill was in the air. Fog was beginning to drift in from the coast, and the temperature of their enthusiasm was dropping fast. For the sake of morale, McBean led them to a nearby saloon for a little spiritual fortification before the ordeal that lay ahead. It was obvious to the resident patrons that this was an army embarking on

a hazardous mission, and questions were asked. Despite orders to
the contrary a few of the men boasted a little, and the name of
Tyler Curtis was mentioned. No one noticed that a local farmer was
sitting alone in a far corner of the saloon taking it all in.

When McBean finally got his men together they staggered out of
town and took the freight road that led to Bodega Corners. Since it
would be a long walk, McBean had them form a column marching
two by two in the paths beaten hard in the road by the horses'
hooves and wagon wheels. Into the cold night the little army
marched toward its mercenary duty. Meanwhile, the man from the
corner of the saloon watched them go, making sure which road
they took. Then he mounted his horse, and taking a lane that
skirted the marchers headed northward to the farms and ranches
lying between Petaluma and Bodega. Paul Revere could not have
been more dedicated to his mission.

It was near daybreak when McBean's army reached the Curtis
ranch house. They were tired, sober, and cold. After coffee and
other necessary stimulants the troops settled down to rest and
await the coming daylight. Meanwhile, on the hills and ridges
surrounding the Curtis ranch, campfires began to blaze up, casting
only tiny circles of feeble light stifled into tiny twinkling spots by
the heavy fog. In eerie contrast, loud voices carried by the damp air
could be heard through the darkness. The lone rider had spread the
alarm, and the settlers had responded to his call; in wagons,
buggies, and on horseback they had come. Old men, young men,
boys in their teens, and even a few women, all armed for battle,
were also waiting for the misty dawn.

At one campfire on the ridge Michael Terry was in command. As
the serious and determined settlers arrived, singly or in little
groups, he dispatched them to strategic positions to block the road
westward to the bay, eastward to the valley towns, and south along
the road over which Curtis's hired guns had traveled. By morning
the Curtis ranch was surrounded by perhaps a hundred men ready
to risk life and limb in defense of their homes. The last to reach

Terry's campfire was the sheriff, still uncertain as to which side he should be on, but hoping somehow to prevent open warfare.

"Howdy, Sheriff," greeted Terry with guarded cordiality. "I thought you'd be showin' up. But to tell the truth of it, I didn't know which side you'd be on. Get down out of yer buggy and come over to the fire and warm yourself. We be all good, honest men here, and we mean no harm to anybody—except them as mean harm to us."

The bulky embodiment of law and order awkwardly descended from the frail buggy that tilted precariously as he alighted and squeaked back to normal balance when relieved of his weight. He came over to the fire and warmed his hands, nodding solemnly to Terry and the circle of men around him. "Well, I ain't here to aid and abet you in whatever you're up to," he declared. "You boys know you hadn't ought to be here. And with guns and all, it looks pretty bad."

"We can see ye, Sheriff, but we can't hear ye. Tyler Curtis has declared war on us, what with his army of hired guns that he's brought in, and them ready to throw us out of house and home. You know we can't just run off with our tails between our legs. So if I was you I'd go down there and try to talk some sense into him, or else get out of the way and let us do what's got to be done." Terry's faithful followers murmured their agreement.

"I've tried to talk to him. Last week he come in, and he said, 'Why haven't you served my papers yet on them squatters?' And I told him, I said, 'Now, Mister Curtis, you know I'm here to carry out the law; but,' I said, 'You can't just throw them people out without giving 'em a chance to pay up or buy you out.' And he said he had his rights under the law, which he does, as you boys well know. And that's the long and the short of it. Now, I don't want no shootin' around here. Somebody might get hurt, and then I'd have to come down on you fellers, and you know I don't want to do that." The sheriff was pleading, not demanding, and the men around the campfire sensed his fear.

"It might not come to shootin' if Curtis will give in," Terry responded. "We've got him outnumbered two to one, and if he's got the sense he was born with he won't start nothing. But if he does, we've got a piece of rope here that will shut him up, and you won't hear no shootin' at all. Now, if you don't want to get mixed up in this, I'd advise you to high-tail it out of here right now. The less you know, the better."

Dawn was breaking, but the fog seemed to thicken. The cold damp air cut through all but the heaviest overcoats, and the faces of the men tingled with the chill of the night. The chirping chorus of the crickets gradually subsided, and a deathlike silence settled over the hillsides except for the occasional melancholy wail of an owl. With the coming of daylight the Curtis ranch buildings slowly took shape, and as they emerged from the mist the watchers from the hills could see smoke curling from the chimneys. The damp air gradually warmed under the autumn sun, and the restless settlers clustered around Michael Terry for orders to action. But just what they were to do next, no one seemed to know.

"We'll have to wait for their first move," Terry cautioned. "Remember, boys, we didn't start it, but if there's a move against us we'll sure as hell finish it." To signify that he meant business, Terry handed to the man standing next to him the rope he had shown the sheriff. It now had a hangman's noose tied into one end, and the man waved it ominously before the crowd.

Leaving their campfires, Terry and his men began to move slowly down toward the Curtis house and outbuildings. There was the stir of life in the yard below, and gradually the makeshift foreign legion from the city began to appear. At McBean's orders they formed an irregular and uncertain line in front of the veranda. Though well armed, somewhat rested, and generously fed, they were reluctant to face open warfare with an organized force of angry settlers.

"This ain't what we bargained for," one of the mercenaries complained.

"You can't back out now," McBean ordered. "So stand your ground, and if shootin' starts dodge behind these trees and ditches, and give 'em hell."

Tyler Curtis emerged from his house, and big Michael Terry, backed by a cohort of his followers, advanced to meet him. The other settlers assembled in a half circle behind them, their guns in plain view and ready for action.

"You can stop right there, Mike," Curtis shouted. "I know why you're here, and it won't do you any good. You are squatters on my land, and you'll either pay up or get out. These men are here on my orders. They'll fight if they have to, but I don't want any bloodshed. And neither do you, I think. So go back peaceably now, or I'll have the law on you."

"Law, is it! I don't see no law here," Terry bellowed. He was right; the sheriff was nowhere to be seen.

"You men are trespassing here!" Curtis was yelling now so they all could hear. "You'll either pay up or get off my property, and that's final."

"Final, is it!" Terry was shouting, too. "I'll tell you what's final. It's the law, is it! Well, such laws are made by the rich and powerful bigwigs just to protect the land-grabbers like you. It's all wrong. Wrong. One man works all his life till he's old and weak and useless, and he's got nothin' to show for it. If my wife gets sick, do you care? If my children go ragged and hungry, do you eat any the less? If these good men, with all their hard work, take hold of the land and make it blossom like the rose, and tend to the cattle and sheep so they multiply and replenish the earth, why should they have to give half of it to you, who never done a bit of work to get your hands dirty. You say this is final, do you! Well, then, let it be final for yourself as well as for us."

The man with the rope advanced and threw it over a sturdy limb of the large oak tree under which they were standing. The well-tied noose dangled a few feet from Curtis. As Terry seized the rope and shook it in Curtis's face, his men tightened the circle around them, their guns raised ready for any sign of interference from the city men. The latter, despite the fact that McBean stood in front of them facing the squatters as a demonstration of defiance and courage, were uncertain as to their role in the affair. They had not come to be shot at, and most of them wanted nothing more than to get out of there and be back on the waterfront in San Francisco. The next moment would certainly determine the course of history. Would there be a lynching, with all its moral and legal consequences? Or would there be a gun battle, with men killed on both sides? One impulsive shot from either side could set off the explosion. Or would there be more talk, with the chance that the issue could be resolved?

Many years afterward, in telling the story to Captain Smith's grandchildren, Curtis said, "Well, I didn't get hanged, as you can see. The squatters had worked themselves out on a limb, and they knew it. We talked some more, and it was finally decided that the squatters that wanted to could buy the land they were on at a price that was reasonable for them, with plenty of time to pay it off. We didn't do too badly on the deal, and we got a steady flow of money to use as capital to develop the ranch we kept. And you can have the satisfaction of knowing that it was your land on which today's schools and churches and towns are now situated. We've not been rich, but we've done well enough, and you'll get your share of what we kept. All in all, I think it worked out for the best."

Many years afterward, in telling the story to his grandchildren, Michael Terry said, "Well, now, that was a merry old donnybrook. There I was, with the settlers backin' me up, tellin' Tyler Curtis to his face what was what, and him with an army of, oh, at least a hundred men with their guns ready to shoot it out with us. A fearful gang of hired guns and cutthroats they were, and us ready to string Curtis up to that old oak tree in his own front yard. Well, he pleaded for his life, and he made us a bargain over the land. He let us farmers and ranchers buy our places at less than half of what they were worth, and on easy terms, too, just to save his skin. So we all come out of it ahead of the game, and some fine day you'll inherit your share of this property that's free and clear and yours accordin' to the law."

Many years afterward in telling the story to his grandchildren, the sheriff said, "This is the way it was. In doin' my duty as the sheriff in those days I was able to prevent a bloody massacre. There they were facing each other, about a hundred and fifty men on each side, with guns blazing and men dodging in and out behind the bushes. The settlers had Curtis with the noose around his neck ready to lynch him right then and there. And I told them, I said, 'Boys, I'm the law here, and I won't stand for no nonsense. I'm the law here, and you can't do that, or I'll come down on you hard. Why don't you just buy the land you're on and settle this thing peaceably?' And I had told Curtis the same thing before that happened, that he should let them buy their places from him, and he took my advice. The battle ended, and the settlers let him go. And that's how I restored law and order in them violent days. Nobody got killed as far as I know, and I never did have to serve them eviction papers, which I knew was all wrong in the first place. So they all owed your old granddad a vote of thanks for stopping the Bodega war, and that's the way the historians ought to remember it."

Lucia and Old Lace

TO THE CITIZENS OF San Francisco in 1863, the little millinery shop near Portsmouth Square was a thing of beauty and a joy to behold. Its tiny windows were always tastefully trimmed with exquisite hats and bonnets of the latest styles. Fine carriages would stop there, and ladies of quality would study the lovely creations and smile approvingly. And their gentlemen wouldn't mind coming along, for there was always the possible pleasure of refined conversation with the charming little lady who ran the shop.

The name by which San Francisco knew her has been forgotten; but her dainty walk, her aristocratic bearing, her enchanting smile, and her friendly manner were well known and appreciated, especially by the young gentlemen, in a city that was troubled by the internal tensions caused by the Civil War. And when she would appear at the dances and balls held at the Presidio, always wearing a most stylish gown and—on the very special occasions—enhancing its beauty with a delicate Irish lace stole over her shoulders, she would never fail to attract attention. Sometimes she wore it as a shawl, sometimes over her head as a scarf; and occasionally, in a mood of gaiety, she would loop it around her neck with one end draping itself in front and the other end falling gracefully over one shoulder. It was a source of great pride and glowing pleasure for whichever young officer was fortunate enough to escort her that evening.

It was not customary for a mere shopkeeper to be discussed in the elegant drawing rooms of the elite of Nob Hill, but this unusual girl was something more than a common tradesperson. There was just enough mystery about her to stimulate—not gossip, for she did nothing to provoke jealousy—chatty speculations. She was obviously a lady of good breeding and therefore worthy of social conversation, particularly since it was considered a mark of good taste for the ladies of high society to be wearing a modish item from her shop.

"She is a widow, you know."

"Oh, yes, poor thing. I hear that her husband was killed in the war. But she bears up well. She'll get over it soon enough, though. She must be only, what would you say, in her twenties?"

"I hear that she doesn't really have to work. She only keeps that shop to take her mind off her troubles. And—haven't you noticed? — she keeps up on what's going on."

The beautiful young shopkeeper did, indeed, know more about current affairs than the more elite ladies of culture needed to concern themselves with, but that was all right for a business woman.

She had come from somewhere "Back East," but she spoke in a manner that was more British than American—with perhaps a faint trace of a southern accent. It was known that she had come across the plains in a wagon train composed of good people who were trying to escape the war.

"I hear that the trip was most miserable for her, poor thing."

"Oh, yes. I think they ran out of provisions on the way and nearly starved to death."

"But that wasn't the worst of it. My husband says that he heard they got lost, or were delayed somehow, and were caught in the winter snows in the mountains like the Donner Party did, only of course they came out all right in the end."

A delicate young girl of refinement who had endured such

hardships could only attract the most sympathetic attention of the male segment of the city, particularly the junior officers at the Presidio, the bankers, and the gentlemen with mining interests, all of whom were willing to give her their advice and offer her other help if she ever needed it. And when the lady appeared at parties or military dances, as she often did, there were plenty of gentlemen, young and old, who were eager to help her adjust that beautiful lace stole around her well-formed shoulders.

What they didn't know was that the lady of the Irish lace had joined the miserable wagon train using a false identity, that her quaint little millinery shop was a fake, and that she was not the sweetly sad widow she pretended to be. She was, in truth, a Confederate spy, and her real name was Lucia Ann Mills. She had been born in Georgia, and hers was a family of quality. She was completely devoted to the Southern cause in the war, and she had been deliberately trained for the job she was to do in San Francisco.

Lucia Ann came from one of the most distinguished families in Georgia. At one time her grandfather had been the third largest landowner and the fifth largest slave holder in the state. In 1852, when her father assumed management of the plantation, he owned hundreds of slaves, but being a liberal man he did not believe in slavery. Educated in England and Scotland, he had become a Whig in politics and was friendly with abolitionists. He had horrified his neighbors, when he took over his father's plantation, by giving many of the slaves their freedom. Lucia Ann bitterly opposed her father's liberal views. It was her old grandfather, a gentleman of the aristocratic South, whom she admired and loved most. So when he urged her to take her father's advice and broaden her education, she went off to a Normal School in Richmond, Virginia. She was eighteen and keenly sensitive to the growing tensions between North and South. She met and even liked several young northerners who were attending a military academy in Richmond, and at their invitation on several occasions visited Washington to attend social affairs, but the southern gentlemen were more her kind. She even attended one social function at West Point. In fact, it was this acquaintance with Northern officers that led to her ultimate downfall in San Francisco.

When the war came, the northern boys went back home, and good riddance. All the members of her family except her father were true to the Old South, and when Georgia seceded the Mills family seceded also. Her three older brothers went into the army to serve the Confederate cause, and the fourth brother would have gone but he was too young. Lucia Ann yearned desperately to do something to help the cause, but what could a mere girl do in the war?

On their way into the service two of her brothers came through Richmond to see her. With them she shared her ardent desire to take an active part in the war, and they encouraged her. Women were needed for various contributions to the struggle, but they had to be carefully selected for special and sometimes dangerous missions. With the help of her brothers she made her plans, and in 1861 she made contact with the Confederate Secret Service. She was readily accepted and assigned to the Treasury Department, but her specific mission was kept secret from her.

Lucia Ann had a very distinct southern accent, but through her association with her British educated father and her closest friend, the daughter of the British Trade Commissioner, she thought she could acquire a more British tone to her speech. For a time the Secret Service had trouble in deciding whether to make her into an English lady or an American woman of the world. They settled for an American lady. She would go to St. Louis to be trained to serve as a gold agent in California. The South desperately needed gold and silver from the western mines to carry on the war, and it was the job of their most clever undercover agents to arrange for clandestine shipments by freight wagons from secret rebel sympathizers to underground points of entry into confederate territory.

Late in 1861 the South still controlled the Mississippi Valley and part of Missouri. Stagecoaches connected the major cities, and ladies could travel freely without interference from the Army. Lucia Ann packed a few of her most necessary things, including her priceless treasure, the Irish lace that had been her grandmother's; it symbolized for her the delicate beauty and gracious living that she admired so much. She was bound for St. Louis, where the training for her secret mission was to be given.

The first problem was her speech. She had to overcome that southern accent. She worked hard, and after months of drilling under the tutelage of a speech teacher she could pass as someone who might have been born in England and educated in Boston. She was also carefully instructed in matters pertaining to mining, finances, freight routes, and the secret connections to be made with the Knights of the Golden Circle, which was an underground network of southern patriots in the West.

She finished school in the middle of 1862, and arrangements were promptly made for her to join a wagon train bound for California. She posed as the daughter of one of the families and was readily accepted as such by other people in the company, but she quickly learned that to maintain such a disguise would not be easy. The hard life of an emigrant girl on the westward trail was something far less glamorous than she had imagined. The journey was indeed miserable, and her later reports of it were so realistic that no one dreamed of doubting her word. She reached San Francisco in the late fall of that year.

With the money she had brought with her Lucia Ann set up as a milliner. The name she assumed will never be known because, when the court house in Richmond was burned, with it went all the records of the Confederate Secret Service. She kept a diary, written in a private code, but it was also destroyed at a later time when the truth was no longer needed or wanted.

In California she had two main assignments. One was to make contact with Southern sympathizers who had access to gold, which she was to collect in small amounts and store in a safe warehouse until shipment to the South could be arranged. To avoid the possibility of its being traced through personal identification with her, the organization chose a place near Monterey for the cache.

When the time was right, the gold was loaded into wagons with false bottoms and shipped to secret destinations in the South.

These gold-laden wagons joined trains going through Arizona to Texas, and when the freight caravan was out of danger from attack by Indians or search by Union troops, the gold wagons would simply break off or get lost and then quietly continue on to their destination. Although most of these wagons took the southern route, some went through Virginia City, picking up more secret cargo there. Often they were even unknowingly escorted by the Federal troops. Wagons going by the northern route went through Iowa, Ohio, and West Virginia—even through the Union lines after the North took the Mississippi Valley.

Lucia Ann's other job was to move in Army circles to gather information about Federal gold shipments and to learn of any that might be carelessly guarded. This information was quickly dispatched to the proper places, and Confederate guerrillas would waylay the wagons and confiscate the gold. Her contact for transmitting information was an undistinguished little man called Ruben, who came and went without suspicion, delivering packages and doing occasional odd jobs around her shop. She took her instructions from him, but where he got his orders she didn't know.

This underground activity was not going unnoticed by the Federal secret agents, who were also good at their business. They had already rounded up and arrested many of the leaders of the Knights of the Golden Circle, and what happened to them was not pleasant to think about. Some were thrown into military prisons and others simply disappeared. California was a long way from Washington, and communication was slow; so people in authority in the West did pretty much as they pleased. What would happen to a woman rebel if she were caught could only be imagined; there was no sympathy for spies and no respect for womanhood in war. Lucia Ann knew that if she were caught she could expect no mercy. She lived in constant fear of being recognized, and grew more careful each day, and more tense. The strain began to tell on her. In

late 1864, her fear was almost unbearable. Perhaps she should quit
before it was too late, she told herself a thousand times.

One night Ruben tapped gently on the back door of her living
quarters behind the shop. "Something's up," he said. "We are not
sure what, but there's something in the wind."

"What's your guess?" she asked.

"I don't know, but it could be a big gold shipment, probably
guarded by the Army. There are some new bluecoats in town. Are
your connections with them still good?"

"Yes, I think so. There's to be a party tomorrow night for some
new colonel, and I have been invited. It will be a grand ball, and
everyone will be there. Somebody might talk." For a moment she
hesitated, thinking of the role she would have to play. The growing
doubts and fears swept through her mind again. "I was thinking,
though," she said, "that I might decline. I haven't been feeling well
lately, and it might be better if I didn't go."

"You must go." From Ruben that was an order, and she knew he
meant it. "Who will be taking you? That young captain who is
falling in love with you?"

"Yes, Captain Arnold," she said. He was a pleasant young man
who had escorted her to several social affairs, and she had grown to
like him. He had always been a proper gentleman, and she was not
pleased with herself for having to use him in this way. If he were
not the enemy, she could easily imagine a life of romance and
happiness with him. But the cause was more important than
personal feelings.

"You must go," Ruben repeated. "Learn all you can about this
new colonel and what he's here for. And especially, find out where
the gold is and how it will be moved, and when. Also we need to
know about the war back home—where the Yankees are and
whether they have cut off any of our lifelines. You know well
enough what to do and how to do it."

She did know. She had done this job often enough before, but
each time became more dangerous. Will this war never end? She

knew it must, one way or another, for the sake of all the people caught in it. Even those damn Yankees must be tired of it by now.

"All right," she said. "I'll go. Be here tomorrow night about midnight and I'll report what I can."

Ruben disappeared as inconspicuously as he had come, and she returned to her work, still troubled by the gamble she was taking. The next day moved through its normal routine, and that evening she dressed in her finest gown. Her young captain arrived on time, and while his carriage waited he busied himself until she was ready by admiring the various items in her shop. Back in her little apartment she slowly and carefully put on the finishing touches. Lovingly she draped the lace around her shoulders and looked at herself in the mirror. At any other time, and if circumstances were different, this would be a pleasure. She drew a deep breath, adjusted her lace wrap, and smiling radiantly turned to meet the young man.

At the ball, the usual officers and their wives paid her the usual compliments. She managed to meet a few new people of influence, and even selected one or two for more confidential conversations later in the evening. Suddenly she felt the presence of another person standing beside her. She turned and cold terror swept over her. She could feel her face turn pale, and her chin trembled a little. There, waiting to be introduced, stood one of her old friends from Virginia, a student who had remained loyal to the North and was now an officer in the Union Army. Captain Arnold, her escort, had led him to her. "May I introduce an old friend of mine who has just come out from Albany? I have the pleasure to present Lieutenant John Miller." As Arnold made the introduction it was obvious that he was delighted in bringing two of his most cherished people together.

She stiffly acknowledged the introduction as if the young man were a stranger. A flash of recognition showed in his eyes. She looked him squarely in the face and extended her hand. "I am delighted to make your acquaintance, sir," she said.

He thought he sensed a look of pleading in her eyes. Something was amiss here, he thought. This would have to be handled

Adjusting her lace wrap, she turned to meet the young officer.

carefully until the situation could be analyzed. With all the chivalry of an officer and a gentleman he took her hand, bowed courteously, and made the polite remarks appropriate to the occasion.

She drifted away in the company of other people, but for the rest of the evening she sensed that he was watching her. At one point, when she was dancing, she saw him talking to a small group of other officers, and then they all turned, ever so casually, to look at her. She knew that time was running out; in a few hours at the most her true identity would be known.

She touched Captain Arnold's arm and said softly, "Could we please leave now? I feel a little faint."

When they reached the shop she quickly got rid of her escort, promising to see him the next evening. She locked the shop door, blew out the lamp in the window, and went through the darkness to her apartment at the rear. It was nearly midnight. Quickly she packed her most necessary things, including the precious lace, into a light bag. This done, she turned the lamp down low and waited for Ruben's gentle tap on the back door. When he came she told him what had happened.

"Dear girl," he said, "you are finished here. By morning this place will be swarming with Yankee agents. There's nothing to do but get you out as fast as possible."

"But the shop?"

"Forget the shop. It has done its work, and so have you. Now listen carefully. I'll take you in my buggy to some friends where you will be safe for a day or two. As soon as possible we'll get you to the warehouse at Monterey. You will be met there, and from that moment on, you will be out of my hands." Everything went as planned. At the warehouse one of her agents met her and arranged for her passage on a British freighter bound for South America. When they reached Panama, Lucia Ann got off and went overland to the Atlantic side, where she found a ship bound for Jamaica. There she had the good fortune to find her uncle, who throughout the war had been a blockade runner. He took her to Savannah, and from there she got home to Cartersville.

She was tired and nervous from her long ordeal of active service, and in her heart there was no forgiveness for the Union. When she saw what the Yankee Army had done to Georgia she became even more bitter. At home she found that her father had been grievously wounded, and shortly afterward he died, an old and beaten man.

The war ended, and her beloved South lay vanquished. Everything she treasured had fallen victim to the North's violence, and those she loved were dead. One brother had been killed in Maryland, and another brother who had been wounded while with Lee's Army in Virginia had come home to die. The third brother, a doctor, had been captured and imprisoned in New York state, where he contracted tuberculosis. And soon after her return the youngest brother had succumbed to diphtheria. She was left alone with what remained of the plantation, and alone she had to run it.

She had to defend herself against the carpetbaggers and hold off the guerrillas, deserters, tax collectors, and returning disillusioned soldiers, and at the same time get the devastated plantation back into cultivation. The fight now was for survival. It was the future that mattered; the past was dead. Her beauty faded into sun-dried wrinkles and calloused hands, and she grew coarse and tough. The gracious past had to be forgotten.

She sat in her rocking chair one evening after a day of hard work, and her thoughts as usual were guided by the bitterness within her. Some things from her past were still in her memory, but the beauty had gone out of them. Like everything else in her old life, they had to die, too. She gripped the arms of the chair and stared straight ahead at the magnolia tree in the yard, and past it on out into space. Then with sudden resolution she rose and went into her bedroom. From a bureau drawer she took out her long hidden secret diary, some old letters, and the soft lace shawl. With a tenderness she had not felt for a long time, she carried them back to her rocking chair and sat fingering them in her lap. The diary brought back into painful reality all the tensions of the war years. It began with hope and the enthusiastic commitment to a cause, and it ended with the echoes of all the conflict and fear and disappointment of a life that was now dead. She thrust it aside as if to cast off an evil spirit. The letters had been saved from her happy school days. She slowly untied the ribbon that held them and seemed to caress each one as she scanned the contents and noted the signatures. Girl friends who had revealed their secret passions and their not so secret foibles, boy friends bursting with enthusiasm and hinting at love—they were all there. Here was the incarnation of a life that had never been quite real, and the people there were now but dream visions. They had served their purpose, but not well enough. She tied the letters together again, and the bundle was tighter in its ribbon than before.

And the lace shawl. Its softness in her hard hands surprised her a little. Here was her gentle grandmother wearing it as she sat on the porch with all the dignity of a queen holding court. Here was her mother for whom the lace had been an heirloom to be kept and treasured but not worn. And here was Lucia Ann proudly showing it off as part of her own delicate charm, a symbol of the heritage that had nurtured vanities and dreams. It had been part of her happiness in youth, it had fought for her and guarded her like a shield in a terrible war, and it had grown old and useless with her in later life.

With a sigh she rose and clasped the three objects to her breast. She walked resolutely to the back yard, picking up some loose papers on the way. There she made a pile as if it were rubbish. Slowly she lit the fire and watched her other life burn to ashes. Then she entered the house and closed the door.

The years passed. She held the plantation together and grew old in the process. Somewhere along the way she married, but there was little love in the union. Life for her was a battle, and she fought it hard. With that delicate lace she had put beauty and love and forgiveness out of her life forever. She died a bitter old woman, hating and being hated.

The Mink Creek Ghost

No one ever found out for sure what happened to the Olsons. There were vague and shadowy rumors and some people suspected foul play, but nothing was ever proved. The curse that fell on the Burrell family, however, was another matter; the facts were obvious to everybody in Mink Creek. The people who were part of it are all dead now, but the story with all its horror still lingers among those of the third generation. It is as if a cold gray fog had settled in that part of the canyon, and even on a clear warm day you might shiver a little when you pass by the old place. All that is left of the house is the desolate ruin of the foundation and a crumbling rock chimney. The people who now own the place work the farm but say they try to avoid trespassing on the spot where the house stood.

Around the turn of this century the Burrells bought the farm from the Olsons. It was situated in the canyon of Mink Creek, which flowed down into Bear River near Preston, Idaho. The Olsons were an old Danish couple who had been converted to the Mormon Church by missionaries and had migrated to America to settle in the New Zion of the West to be near the brethren of their faith. They had settled on the farm in the canyon and seemed to be making a modest living from it.

They built the house and put a shed or two nearby to protect their three milk cows and a few sheep from the winter snows, and another shed for the two horses that dragged the plow or did other heavy work six days of the week and pulled the wagon to take the old folks to church on Sundays. Their big black dog, vicious and menacing to all strangers, but faithful to the old couple, slept in the house by the fireplace.

A few years passed and the Olsons, though comfortable enough as far as their physical needs were concerned, were never entirely happy. They missed their native language and the warm companionship of their friends in the old country. The things they had been willing to leave behind for the sake of their new religion gradually grew into sadly sweet memories that kept calling them home. At last they decided to sell out and go back to Denmark.

Their neighbor, a man named Burrell, bought the farm. He borrowed the money in order to pay them in cash as they demanded, and the deal was made. Apparently the title and deed were in good order, and the Olsons departed. The livestock went with the place and the dog, it was assumed, had died either of old age or by some private means that was nobody's business. Parley Burrell, a taciturn and moody man, occasionally generous but mostly hard-fisted and miserly, apparently as a gesture of good will offered to drive them down to Cache Junction on the day of their departure to see them off. When they left the canyon the old couple had only their luggage and of course the cash that Burrell had paid them. They were never heard from again.

Burrell with his wife and three daughters—Helen, Betsy, and Carrie—moved into the Olson home and set to work running the farm. The girls, all in their teens, were good looking, popular in school, and at home helpful with the many chores to be done. Burrell worked hard, kept to himself except when circumstances forced him to associate with his neighbors, and avoided the usual church activities in the small community. He was also different in another very minor way; he and his family had no pets. Most farm households kept cats and dogs, but not the Burrells. The girls, in particular, disliked dogs.

"I'm so glad the Olsons didn't leave that big, ugly, black dog for us to take care of," Helen remarked one day. "You remember, Papa, how he snarled and almost bit me once. I hate him."

"Don't worry," the father said. "He can't hurt you now. He's dead."

"Did you kill him, Papa?" little Carrie wanted to know.

"Yes." And the matter was dropped.

The days glided into months, the farm went through its seasons, and a year passed. One evening in late November when the cool nights of autumn were beginning to take on the chill of coming winter, the family sat together by the fireplace after supper. The girls were at the kitchen table studying their lessons for school, with the lamp in the center casting ample light for reading but fading out to dark shadows in the corners of the room. Their parents sat silently on either side of the fireplace just resting, watching the flames in the grate, and waiting for bedtime.

A wind was beginning to blow down the canyon. It seemed to gather force with incredible suddenness, and they could hear the sound of it rising to a high-pitched howl. At that time of year a night wind was not unusual, but this seemed to be something different. It increased in power until it became an unmistakable wail like a human cry. It hissed through the cracks in the rafters and moaned around the window sills like a lost soul calling from the grave.

The flames in the fireplace burned lower. The kerosene lamp weakened gradually, and with a little flutter it went out, leaving the room in darkness except for the feeble red glow from the hearth. Suddenly there was a scream, and someone fell to the floor. Immediately the wind died down, the flames in the fireplace revived, and the lamp flickered into light again. In the center of the room the oldest daughter lay dead. Her throat had been torn open by something that left fang marks, and there were scratches on her face.

The whole community joined the family in their grief, and the beautiful young body was buried with the usual Mormon tenderness and sympathy. Questions were asked, of course, but there were no answers that made sense. The coroner in particular had a problem; no murder suspect could be found, so the gruesome death was quietly attributed to "a person or persons unknown." The Burrells grieved, and that part of the farm crop which had not yet been harvested was killed by an early frost.

Months passed and the Burrells had managed to put out of their minds the acuteness of the tragedy. Fall and winter came again, and in the evenings as usual the family settled down after supper to catch the warmth of the glowing logs in the fireplace. On this particular night Mr. Burrell felt like talking about what had been on his mind all day. "I guess it was about a year ago," he said, "that Helen—"

"Just one year today," his wife said. She, too, had been thinking of it. Betsy and Carrie looked at each other, but neither could think of anything to say.

"Seems like the wind is coming up again," Burrell continued. "It gets worse this time of year."

The night wind was sweeping down the canyon growing stronger and more insistent by the moment. Once again that howling voice seemed to circle the house like a wild creature trying to get in. The older daughter began to tremble.

"Help me, Papa!" she cried.

The log fire suddenly burned low, the lamp dimmed, and the room was dark. A piercing scream cut through the darkness. When the fire rose and light again filled the room, Betsy lay dead on the floor. Something had gouged her throat.

Again the whole town shared in the grief of the family, but this time there was fear as well. Something not of this world had come upon the place. The belief in supernatural powers was close to the Mormons of that time and place, and it was well known that the forces of evil, nourished in sin, could manifest themselves in terrible ways. In this case there could be no doubt. Someone had sinned, and this was the punishment. Burrell was questioned most thoroughly. Had he blasphemed God? No. Had he done harm or injustice to anyone? No. Had he hurt the Olsons in any way? No. Had he fully paid for the farm? Yes. Burrell was not much of a talker, and sometimes his words were blunt, his manner surly. Neighbors now began to remember that he had a mean streak in him. He could be cruel to animals. He did not come to church, and he paid no tithing. He always drove a hard bargain, and he pinched his pennies. Where did he get the money to pay off the debt on the farm? Had he heard from the Olsons since they left?

His answers were always short, and he volunteered no information. But nothing could be turned up that would implicate him in the two violent murders. Obviously, then, it was some supernatural power at work here. The fears of the community were heightened by the unquestioned conviction that devils could and frequently did frustrate the affairs of man. But also, by the power of the priesthood, evil spirits could be cast out. Their duty became clear to the elders of the church; they must do their best to protect the stricken family and the entire community.

As the year went by, apprehension increased. Little Carrie was clearly in great danger and so was the town, for if this were indeed the work of the Devil everyone shared in the curse. Plans were quietly made, and on the anniversary of the two fatal events several men from adjacent farms came to the Burrell home. One, the Mormon Bishop, "administered" to the girl by anointing her head with oil, and by the "laying on of hands" invoked the blessings of God for her protection and safety. The other men sat in a circle around little Carrie to shield her from whatever earthly or demonic force might try to break through.

The evening slowly moved toward midnight. Mr. and Mrs. Burrell sat beside each other near the fireplace holding hands for mutual comfort. The men of the priesthood had finished their prayers and sat in their circle silently waiting, staunch in the faith that God was on their side. He would not let this awful thing happen again, and their "testimony in the church" would be strengthened. The girl trembled in fear. The waiting and the silence were unbearable.

Again the wind began to rise. Its fierceness increased until the whole house seemed to shudder. The low moan outside the window rose to a screeching howl. The flames in the fireplace died down leaving only the red coals of the wood in the grate, and a gust of air blew into the room. The lamp went out and the room turned black. The scream that echoed into the night was the frail girl's last desperate cry.

When light was restored, the father was gone. He had run out into the night. Later when he was found, thrashing through the brush along the creek, he was babbling something about the Olsons. No one could be sure whether his confession was real or imaginary; but if, as he said, he had murdered the Olsons, stolen their money, and buried them somewhere in the canyon, there was no evidence. Some thought these were the delusions of the demented brain of a man in anguish. Others believed that the ghosts of Mr. Olson and his dog had returned for vengeance and that God had denied the innocent girls the protection of their religion because the sins of the fathers are visited upon their children. For many, that was evidence enough.

Mr. Burrell died in an institution, and Mrs. Burrell sold the farm and moved away. The house, it is said, mysteriously caught fire one night and burned to the ground leaving only the foundation and chimney that can be seen to this day. A few years after all this happened, two skeletons were uncovered where workmen were digging for the foundation of the Lewiston Sugar Factory, but they were never identified.

Unto Her a Child Was Born

IT MUST HAVE BEEN June when Rebecca came to live with Uncle George and Aunt Betty. To Earl and Homer this was big news, and the fact that word of her coming was slow in getting around made it all the more interesting. There were only ten families in the community, and when a stranger came to town everybody knew it, sometimes well ahead of the visitor's arrival. But Rebecca was a surprise. All of a sudden there she was. Where she had come from, no one knew—Parowan, Cedar City, St. George, or even further away. Aunt Betty was unusually vague about that. Those who saw her reported that she was apparently in her mid-twenties, which to Earl and Homer made her middle-aged, and she was not particularly good looking. She was just a stranger from out of town and therefore an object of great curiosity.

Hatton was a little farming hamlet between the Pahvant Mountains and the Black Rock Desert in western Utah. The farmers made a marginal living in a place where children were an asset—until they grew up and went away and were replaced by the process of reproduction. In Earl's family there were eleven, but that was felt by some critics to be going a bit too far. Uncle George and Aunt Betty were the only couple without offspring, but they did not lack for helping hands; several youngsters in Hatton were willing

76

to help them out whenever the need arose. They were really Earl's uncle and aunt, but everybody in town, even the old folks, called them Uncle George and Aunt Betty.

It was strange, therefore, that at this time in their lives the old couple would take in a boarder. George Whitaker had been a true pioneer. As a lad he had crossed the plains in a covered wagon; he had herded cows on the communal meadow that later became the municipal square in Salt Lake City; and when he grew up he had applied for and received a Federal land patent, along with a few others, for his homestead acres in the valley of Corn Creek, which later got the name of Hatton.

The boys always enjoyed being around him for the stories he could tell about the early days. One yarn almost believable was about when George's mother had made him a pair of rawhide buckskin breeches. He wore them when he went out to herd cows, and one day a rainstorm came up. When they got wet those trouser legs began to stretch. They got longer and longer, and he kept cutting them off so he wouldn't trip over himself. Finally it stopped raining, the sun came out, and those breeches began to dry. As they dried they shrank until the legs had shortened to his knees. "When I walked I looked like I was always on the jump," Uncle George chuckled. Well, this could have happened. The boys always went barefoot in the summer, and the soles of their feet grew tough like the pads of a dog's paw. But Uncle George said that was nothing. Why, when he was a boy his feet were so tough he could stamp out a cactus and even strike sparks from a rock when he kicked it. Homer could manage to walk barefooted on alfalfa stubble if necessary, but when he tried to kick sparks from a rock it didn't work. Maybe Uncle George had stretched that a little.

For the farmers in Hatton life followed the cycles of the land. The time for sowing and the time for reaping set the boundaries of their existence. Their animals, too, were a harmonious part of this revolving pattern of the seasons. So in late July the cows were calving, the sows were having their litters, and the little turkeys were growing up. In the fields the wheat was sprouting heads of grain and the corn was in the tassel.

At Uncle George's place one Sunday afternoon Earl and Homer had wandered in to sample the wild plums that grew along the ditch banks and, incidentally, to see if they could get a glimpse of the stranger, Rebecca. To make everything seem natural, Earl casually remarked, "Your corn's shore growin' tall."

"That ain't nothing," Uncle George snorted. "Why, back in Ioway the corn really did grow like thunder." Then by way of verification he began to render a hoarse, rasping song that tried to fit into the tune of "Yankee Doodle" with variations:

> "Oh, the corn it grew to be forty-foot high,
> So thick we couldn't number.
> The stalks we used for our house logs,
> The leaves we used for lumber!"

The boys thought that was pretty good. But even better, they did get to visit a little with Rebecca.

In August the crops were growing according to the rules of nature, and so was curiosity about Rebecca and why she was there. Any stranger who came to visit in Hatton had to undergo an implicit social examination to be accepted. The good people of the community may have had their prejudices, but in this isolated and tranquil world such social attitudes did not reach the surface. A stranger's place of origin or even religion did not seriously alter the unexpressed criteria for acceptance, although to be a Mormon might help a little to compensate for other shortcomings in character. After all, little old Sarah Guernsey, who had come from "somewhere way back East" to teach in the one-room school, was not of the Church, but she was accepted and admired, particularly for her discipline in school. More than once Earl and Homer had felt the sting of her ruler.

Rebecca, though she did not participate in the social life of the town, not even to the extent of going to Sunday School, was also accepted. "She ain't stuck up, or nothin' like that," Earl declared, expressing the general view of the community.

But then something new came to light. It was in late August when word got around that Rebecca was "in a family way." Earl was breathless with excitement as he spread the gossip. "She got knocked up, and she come over here to have it so nobody wouldn't find out about it."

Mrs. Stowe had said, "Somebody got at her, and he ought to marry her or she should have the law on him." That was a well-established dogma in the mores of the community, and the pronouncement that some girls "had to get married" was familiar to all. Whenever a couple were married in the region, Earl always counted on his fingers up to nine, which then became the month of biological prediction. Also when a first child was born to a newly wedded couple Earl would count backwards from nine to see whether nature and the social event were in accord. Earl loved a scandal. In the case of Rebecca, however, he was for the time being frustrated because he could not know either the beginning or the end of the developing story.

Since the people of Hatton lived close to the soil, all the children were well schooled in the processes of reproduction from start to finish. They had all observed and even assisted in fertilization, conception, gestation, and birth; and of course this knowledge about the animal world was projected to the human sphere as well. But there were still mysteries to be solved and uncharted territories to be explored. Lorin Stowe's sister Ava and Earl's younger sister Olive were of an age to be paired socially with Homer and Earl, and since they were the only girls in town of that age it was naturally assumed that they should "run together."

Kissing games at parties were very popular for all ages, and Homer found Ava's kisses soft and enthusiastic, but since Olive was Earl's sister the structure of the foursome's relationship was established for them. Homer didn't mind, however; Olive was more fun to be with, anyway.

The girls, of course, never talked of sexual matters. At least, not around the boys. They even blushed a little and looked the other way when Rebecca's condition was mentioned. "She'll be having a baby without a papa," Earl had said, intrigued by this unusual development in human affairs. The girls kept their thoughts to themselves. These circumstances prompted Homer's stepfather to bring up a subject that hitherto had been taboo. There were, he explained, certain kinds of women in the outside world. There were "scarlet women," "women of the street," and "women of easy virtue," and the general admonition was to keep away from them. A rich man might have his "fancy woman," but such misguided creatures were also to be avoided as well as pitied. Mr. Stowe was somewhat less euphemistic; he used the ugly word "whore." Such women, he was pleased to point out, were "a necessary evil." For him the phrase struck the right balance between worldliness and morality. "A necessary evil," he repeated.

But everybody in Hatton agreed that Rebecca was not one of these. She was obviously a good girl who had been wronged. Uncle George and Aunt Betty were doing a good thing by taking her in, and her not even related to them at all. Earl and Homer watched her changing condition with fascination. "She's beginning to swell a little," Earl observed after a visit to his uncle's farm in September.

The potatoes were now ready to dig, and Uncle George needed help. Usually Aunt Betty worked in the field with him, but this year, what with Rebecca around, she declined to contribute that kind of labor. But Earl was more than willing to step into the breach.

"I and Homer can help you," he volunteered.

"For one day or two maybe I could use you." Uncle George seemed none too eager to have both boys; they played as much as they worked. "One boy's a boy; two boys, half a boy; three boys, no boy at all," he declared with great wisdom. Nevertheless, he hired both boys for fifty cents a day to follow the furrows that the plow made as it brought up the potatoes and laid them bare along the folded soil. They picked up these fruits of the earth and put them in buckets which, when full enough to be heavy, they emptied into sacks piled in the shade of a nearby tree. Earl in particular was eager for this job because he wanted to get a good look at Rebecca "to see how far along she was."

Two or three times the boys maneuvered the chance to talk with Rebecca. Earl tried to "pump" her for whatever information he could get as to the origin of her condition, but she did not reveal her secrets and the mystery only deepened. She was a sweet and gentle person, and the boys liked her; they agreed in the assumption that she had suffered in some past experience that was not her fault. And once, when she had said, "I like it here. I think God must have sent me to this place," her words became a kind of clue for them. If God had sent her, there must be something special about her. Then they remembered that when they had first seen her she was wearing a thin blue scarf.

"Just like the picture of the Virgin Mary in the Bible," Earl had said. This coincidence was too significant to overlook. God had sent the Virgin Mary to Bethlehem for the birth of little Jesus, and they remembered from Sunday School that Jesus was supposed to return to the world for the "millennium," whatever that was; so He would have to get born again, wouldn't he? This awesome thought reminded the boys of something else she had said. When Earl, in one of their conversations with her, had brought the subject around to something about having a baby, she had remarked that the birth of a child was one of God's miracles. This was a profound thought. The cause and effect relationships involved in this reproduction of their livestock and even the whole process in the birth of their own brothers and sisters were normal and natural events. But in Rebecca's case it was a miracle. There was something different going on here.

By October the corn had been harvested, the wheat had been cut, bound in bundles, and put into stacks to await the coming of the threshing machine, and the summer fruits and vegetables had been bottled for winter use. And Rebecca was, as Earl put it, "pretty bulgy now." The missing parts of his finger-counting equation were beginning to come into place. "It'll be in December," he predicted. Homer held out for January, but he wasn't sure.

In November the thresher came and the wheat was stored in bins in the granaries. Pigs were butchered, hams were cured, bacon sides were salted and stacked away, and the fat was "tried out" and rendered into lard for the winter. The corn was harvested, shucked, and ready to be shelled. The land had given birth, and what it brought forth was good. Earl and Homer had put on their new shoes for the new school year and had become reasonably well adjusted to the mental tasks required of them in Miss Guernsey's one-room schoolhouse. And Rebecca was well along toward fulfilling her earthly destiny.

"I bet it's goin' to happen about Christmas," Earl said.

"Maybe," Homer conceded.

"What if it happened on Christmas Day!" Earl was awed by the meaning inherent in this sudden thought. "If it come on Christmas wouldn't that be something!" This was not a question but the declaration of a profound truth.

"Like little Jesus!" Homer exclaimed, caught by the excitement of it. By mid-December the birth was clearly imminent. The women of the town began to assume their proper roles as Sisters in the Church. Sister Rollins dropped in with some tiny knitted things left over from her last infant some years before. Sister Robinson bought some cloth and made a stack of diapers for their inevitable practical use. Sister Whitaker, Earl's mother, would have contributed something but she was expecting a twelfth for herself and didn't have anything to spare. Sister Bird let it be known that she was standing by to render help in midwifery, a service in which she had some experience. And Aunt Betty was aflutter with anticipation. It seemed that everybody had something to offer on this holy occasion but Earl and Homer.

"Why don't we give it a present?" Earl suggested. "It bein'

Christmas, and all, I think we ought to. We could look in the Sears and Roebuck or the Monkey Ward catalog for something nice."

"I ain't got no money," said Homer. "And anyway, there ain't time."

"If it come on Christmas, it would be just like little Jesus and the Virgin Mary, and we ought to bring gifts," Earl went on.

"I could shoot some cottontail rabbits and give them for their Christmas dinner," Homer suggested.

"No, not that. The wise men didn't bring food; they brought other stuff. Say, what if she really is the Virgin Mary come in disguise just to test us. Wouldn't that be something!"

"Well, she can't be the Virgin Mary. Her name's Rebecca."

"But maybe she could be." Earl was thinking fast now. "Ain't Rebecca the name of somebody out of the Bible? Anyway, we could play like she was the Virgin Mary."

An idea had germinated and taken root. The next Sunday Earl and Homer looked through the Sunday School books stored in a cabinet in one corner of the schoolhouse. They found a Bible with colored pictures of the Saints, and, sure enough, there was the Mother with the Child cradled in her arms. She was wearing a bright blue robe, and He was swaddled in white. It was an inspiring scene.

"Look, they've both got yellow circles over their heads," observed Earl, a little perplexed by this phenomenon.

"That's because they are holy," Homer explained from the depths of his more scholarly education. Then a new thought came to them. It must have been a divine inspiration. They remembered a song from Sunday School about this very thing: "Away in a manger, no crib for a bed,
    The little Lord Jesus laid down his sweet head."

"What she needs is a cradle," Earl mused, awed by the thought. "The little Lord Jesus didn't have a cradle, did he?"

"He had a manger, but I don't know about no cradle." Homer's classical knowledge did not reach that far.

"Well, we could play like she needed a cradle. I know—let's make it a cradle for Christmas."

This new and inspiring idea seemed feasible enough. The boys went to Homer's stepfather's workshop and immediately set about their awesome task. They sawed and hammered and nailed and carved until the finished product was a joy to behold. It was a longish box mounted on rockers that let it sway from side to side. The head end was slightly higher than the foot, and nailed to the center of this headboard was a handle that stuck up a foot above the cradle. It was like a lever to be pulled back and forth to make the cradle rock. When finished, this piece of workmanship was a creation fit for a god.

"Now we've got to paint it up nice and pretty," Earl declared. "We'll take it up to my place; I know where there's some leftover paint."

"What color? It ought to be some kind of Christmas color," Homer said.

"Yeah. Let's make it red and green."

So that is the way it turned out. Which predominated, the red or the green, would be difficult to determine, but the result was brilliant. At last it was finished to their satisfaction, and the boys hid it away to await the event that would signal its unveiling.

The days passed, and Christmas was approaching. In every home the usual preparations were being made. Shapely juniper trees had been hauled in from where they grew at the edge of the western desert and were firmly erected in one corner of the area that served as the "front room." They were decorated with loops of popcorn threaded on long strings, and to add color there were strands of chain-linked slips of paper, red, green, and white. Small candles were clipped to the branches, and brightly colored glass balls and other ornaments were hung among the boughs. Small packages took their place on the floor amid the cotton snow under the tree, and the larger gifts—a new sled, for instance—leaned patiently against the wall nearby. The spirit of Christmas was descending on the little town of Hatton.

On the day before Christmas Eve the word went out that Rebecca was having her baby. Earl was openly disappointed. "It shouldn't come till tomorrow, or maybe on Christmas Day," he complained. Nature had not followed the ordained scheme of things. But everything else in town went according to its annual schedule. Thick, heavy clouds had settled in, and a snow was predicted. The usual big Christmas party was to be held this year at Ava's house and the whole town was invited. Even though no invitations were issued, everybody knew that whoever wanted to come would be expected and welcome; the only question ever asked was where the party was to be. Everyone brought refreshments, and young and old mixed in the festivities with equal pleasure.

During the party word came that Rebecca had had her baby. It was a boy. Everything was fine. Earl and Homer now had a personal stake in the event even though their Christ child should have waited a day or two. It was clear that celestial beings could choose their own time to manifest themselves.

That night the snow came and continued through the next day. By Christmas morning the skies had cleared and the streams had frozen over. Nearly a foot of snow had fallen, and the younger folk issued forth to join in such winter sports as snowball fights and sled riding. An old horse was brought out to pull the half dozen sleds that hitched on like a train behind him to make the smooth ride up and down the one road that threaded the town together. The barrow pit that paralleled the road had been flooded with water diverted from the irrigation ditch, and the surface of this long boy-made lake was frozen solid. Boys and girls arrayed in colored scarfs, toboggan caps, and mittens glided up and down the narrow strip of ice, racing each other and occasionally colliding into a heap of sprawling arms and legs and screeching voices.

That afternoon Earl and Homer decided it was time to go and see the new baby. Their present was still a secret, so when nobody was around to see them they fastened the cradle to Earl's sled and dragged it up to Uncle George's house. On the way Earl got a new idea. "I wonder what she's goin' to name it."

"I don't know. What difference does that make?"

"Well, this bein' a Christmas baby, and all that, it seems like she ought to name it Jesus."

"They don't nobody name their kids Jesus any more. That's just for Mexicans and such," explained Homer, not yet entirely convinced that Earl's intuition was infallible. "Well, if she don't name it Jesus, maybe she could name it something like Christopher. That's pretty close even if it wasn't born in a manger. And ain't we coming like the wise men to bring it a present?"

"There was three of them wise men," Homer protested. "We ain't but just two."

"We could play like we was the three wise men."

And so the magi arrived bearing their gift, ready to pay sacred homage to the newborn infant of Christmas. Aunt Betty met them at the door and ushered them into the holy place.

"I and Homer have come to see the new baby," Earl said, "and here's a present that we brought."

They reverently entered the chamber that was Rebecca's room. She was sitting up in bed with pillows stuffed behind her. In her arms lay the newborn child, but it didn't look very much like the holy infant of the Bible picture. Rebecca was not wearing a shining blue robe, and the baby did not have the round cherubic face they expected; its eyes were shut, and its tiny face was wrinkled, more like an old man's. Nor were there any golden circles over its head or Rebecca's.

Earl presented the cradle with self-conscious modesty. "Here's this cradle from I and Homer; we thought maybe you could use it." he said.

Rebecca smiled as she looked at the unusual gift. "That's real nice of you," she said. "Thank you, Earl. Thank you, Homer."

The boys felt a thrill of satisfaction. The gift of the magi had been accepted. But one question remained. If any sign were to come from Heaven, now was the time.

"What are you goin' to name it?" Earl asked. The final test of divinity was at hand. The boys waited.

Rebecca looked at them a long time, and she slowly said, "I'm going to name him Henry."

Death Valley Scotty

SAINT PETER WAS RELAXING, as usual, in his easy chair down by the Pearly Gates. For centuries he had been sitting around with nothing to do but screen the applicants for admission to Paradise. Business had been slow of late, and the work was pretty dull except when some unusual character happened along to break the monotony. The result was obvious: 1954 was simply not a vintage year for world obituaries, at least for souls that had any flair. Peter's old friend Lucifer seemed to be getting the edge on the competition; the really attractive people went his way.

He tried to doze off, but some of the more evangelistic angels were making too much noise with their hymns and hallelujah choruses, and he couldn't sleep. He had intended at least a thousand times to speak to the Archangel about that. A little fervor was all right, but this younger generation were altogether too loud. Not like the good old days. Suddenly this reverie was interrupted by a loud banging at the gate. Peter sat up with a start, adjusted his heavenly robes, and leaned over to activate the celestial computer at his side. This device of divination immediately processed the ill-mannered soul at the gate and obediently printed out the identification: SCOTT, WALTER E. . . . ALSO KNOWN AS DEATH

VALLEY SCOTTY ... CALIFORNIA ... BORN KENTUCKY, 1872 ...

Peter pushed another button, and a strange apparition materialized before him. It wore a black Stetson hat, blue flannel shirt, flaming red tie, and heavy leather boots—not exactly the expected costume of a conventional personage this late in the century. The guardian saint studied his colorful visitor for a moment. "So you are the famous Death Valley Scotty," he said appraisingly.

"That's me. In the flesh—that is, in a manner of speaking, as you might say. I'm the best damn publicity man you ever saw, and with plenty of dough to prove it." With this, he pulled a roll of fifty-dollar bills from his boot and tossed them at the feet of the startled saint.

"Your money is hardly a recommendation for getting into Heaven. Up here it is just so much paper to dispose of. Litter, you know."

"Yeah, well I hear that you have streets of gold, and golden harps and halos and things like that. So you need me." Scotty was beginning to warm up on his favorite pitch. "I've got a big gold mine in Death Valley that can supply you with all you want."

"Now hold on there. You just wait one extra-terrestrial minute. Your gold mine is a fake and we all know it. If you don't tell the truth around here you won't have a ghost of a chance of getting into Heaven." Peter always enjoyed that little joke, but it was wasted on Scotty. "If you want to get in here you'll have to tell the truth, the whole truth, and nothing but ..."

"That'll come hard for me," said Scotty, somewhat crestfallen at such a prospect. "I don't think I ever told the truth in my life—and that's a fact—except once or twice, and it always got me in trouble."

"Only the truth," warned the saint. "Why don't you try, anyway?" Peter was beginning to be amused by this fellow. His right to be in Heaven was extremely doubtful, but if he could make a good case maybe his presence would stir things up a little.

The celestial computer began to click again in anticipation of the scenario to come. ASK HIM ABOUT HIS IMAGINARY GOLD MINE ... HIS FAMOUS SPEED RECORD ON A SANTA FE TRAIN ...

THE BATTLE OF WINGATE PASS ... THE CASTLE IN DEATH
VALLEY ...

As Scotty told his story, his rather too colorful words were
translated into more comprehensible and appropriately orthodox
language by the omniscient instrument. The print-out is still on file
in the Paradisical Archives, and it is from that document that this
legend comes.

Death Valley Scotty was a man who knew well how to attract the
attention of the public and make his name a household word. He
would, as he once said, "Always play to the gallery. The better it
sounds, the better they like it." He captured the public imagination
with his flair, his style, his wit, and his sense of timing, and he
became a consummate artist in public relations. While he was
never a rich man, he pretended to be one. He created for himself
a legend and then proceeded to live it.

He was born Walter E. Scott in Cynthiana, Kentucky, on
September 20, 1872, the youngest of six children. Scott's father
raised and trained trotting horses, and Walter traveled the harness-
racing circuit with him. He got little formal schooling, but he did
acquire a taste for life on the road and learned the riding skills that
later made him into a showman and a living legend.

At age eleven Scotty left Kentucky and headed west to Nevada
to join his older brothers who were working as ranch hands. It isn't
clear how or exactly when he came to California—Scotty never told
the same story twice about that. Apparently at the age of sixteen he
was an apprentice wrangler for awhile, and then he got a job as a
water boy for a survey party running a state boundary line between
California and Nevada. There he got his first glimpse of Death
Valley.

In 1890 a talent scout signed him on as a cowboy performer with
the Buffalo Bill Wild West Show, where he met Major John Burke,
who was an expert in publicity. From him Scotty learned that the
legend is more important than the man himself. Burke and the
adventure story writer Ned Buntline published two highly
fictionalized accounts about Buffalo Bill that were the foundation of

his rise to fame. They turned William Cody, frontiersman, into Buffalo Bill, an international celebrity. Scotty was with the Buffalo Bill show twelve years, during which he learned all the tricks of showmanship. He traveled two continents, developed a taste for the roar of the crowd, and learned that people are always willing to pay for a good show. The Kentucky farm boy was gradually transformed into a self confident and assured man of the world without any compunction about deceiving people who wanted to be fooled.

In the 1890's gold was big business in the West, so Scotty decided to learn about gold. In 1900 he married Ella Josephine Milius from New York City. They came west, and he worked in the mines of Cripple Creek, Colorado. One day Mrs. Scott was taken into a mine to see how the work was done, and as a souvenir the superintendent gave her two samples of ore. These mementos were to become the next eggs for Scotty's subsequent career.

In 1902 he was back with the Wild West Show, which was scheduled to open in New York City. Scotty was late for the grand opening, so Cody docked him two weeks' pay. Scott's pride was hurt, and he quit the show. But to be in New York without a job was intolerable. Here was a challenge that called for genius. He tapped his greatest resource, his imagination, and the inspiration came. That same afternoon he went to his rooms and took from his wife's handbag the two samples of gold ore. He slipped them into his pocket and went off to see the prosperous Julian M. Gerard of the Knickerbocker Trust Company.

To the city banker he spun a fanciful tale of gold to be found in Death Valley. Gerard was interested. Yes, he had heard of Death Valley. Scott knew a secret place where there was gold. He had a fabulously rich claim, and here were the ore samples to prove it. Gerard's eyes glittered. All Scott needed was a grub stake for which the banker could own a share of the mine. The samples were rich, the story was good, and Gerard was greedy—a perfect combination. Scott came away with a handsome grub stake and a partner in a mine that existed only on paper.

Thus begins the legend of Death Valley Scotty's gold mine. He returned to Death Valley and became, at least on paper, a prospector. He never bought any tools and never shipped any ore. He spent most of his time in saloons, but he did find the time to explore the desert. Eventually he made his headquarters at the head of a narrow canyon identified on current maps as Scotty's Canyon. He called it "Camp Holdout," and for five years he sent reports to Gerard describing the progress he was making. In every letter he was just within reach of the big lode, and he always asked for more money. But privately he said, "What the hell's the use lookin' when somebody already found the good ones." So he didn't bother to look. His rich vein was Gerard.

In 1904 there was a gold strike at Tonopah and Goldfield just north of Death Valley. Scotty used this news to promote himself. He sent out a press release to the effect that a pillow case containing gold dust belonging to him and valued at $12,000 had been stolen, but he was quoted as saying that the loss was insignificant. "There's plenty more where that came from," he bragged.

His story made front page news in all the major papers. To prolong this wave of publicity Scotty went on a carefully planned spending spree in Los Angeles with eager reporters following him around. His distinctive costume of a blue flannel shirt, flaming red tie, and Stetson hat, plus the big roll of bills he flashed everywhere, created a character the public loved. One reporter for the Los Angeles *Examiner* wrote a series of feature stories about this flamboyant Death Valley Scotty, and the readers hungrily begged for more. No movie star could have asked for better publicity.

There was much speculation as to the source of Scotty's money. Back in New York City, Gerard heard about the wild spending spree and began to wonder why some of this sudden wealth was not coming his way as a shareholder in the mine. The icing on the joke, of course, was that it was Gerard's money being spent. "It was runnin' old Gerard nuts," cackled Scotty later. "He thought I had a secret mine, and so did everybody else. You should of seen them shills bug their eyes out when I'd throw a handful of twenties all over the house."

But Gerard was no fool. He repeatedly asked Scotty for his share and was always put off. The mine needed more tools, more supplies, more working capital. When Gerard asked to be shown the mine, excuses were made. Such a trip would be too dangerous— wild Indians, outlaws, claim jumpers, land slides, and whatever else might discourage an investigation. At last Gerard was convinced that Scott was a fake, and his financial support dried up.

Clearly it was time to attract more investors. Now, let's see. Who else needed publicity big enough to arouse thewhole country? Well, the Santa Fe railroad was in the doldrums; its stock was sinking and it needed a new image. This was 1905 now, and the public would demand something more spectacular than a shower of twenty-dollar bills; people wanted speed to match the modern age. So Scotty devised a scheme. He would charter a Santa Fe train and, breaking all records in a death-defying stunt, would drive the train at a speed beyond its limits in a race against time from Los Angeles to Chicago.

With some "up front" expense money—Scotty said $10,000, but the records show $5,000—he leased a train. At noon on July 9th, with the crowds cheering and Scotty at the throttle, the Coyote Special pulled out of the Los Angeles station. All other trains were cleared from the line, and at every town along the way the people came to watch. With black smoke streaming and piston rod throbbing, the big locomotive hugged the rails and strained with all its power, streaking across the desert wastes like a demon out of hell, dragging its little train behind. With the long wail of the whistle and the hissing of steam it tore through the towns and was gone before the cheering crowds could even count its cars. It reached Chicago on July 11th after just forty-four hours and forty-four minutes, setting an incredible speed record. In Chicago Scotty was a hero, and the tale of the Coyote Express became a legend.

Since no more money was coming from Gerard, Scotty had to find a new patron. With the Chicago publicity this was easy. He met and charmed an insurance magnate, Albert M. Johnson, a millionaire in poor health who was willing to take a chance on Death Valley. As Scotty later said, "There was Johnson with his checkbook, and that was easier than diggin' gold even on top of the ground." And the beauty of it was that Johnson didn't seem to care whether there was a mine or not. He visited Scotty in Death Valley and found the place good for his health, and that was what mattered.

But Scotty's past was about to overtake him. Gerard and a few other Eastern partners would not stay where they belonged. They demanded to see the mine in which they owned a share, and a party of them including Gerard set out to make a firsthand inspection of the property. They were led by A. Y. Pearl, a mining promoter who had interested a syndicate in investigating Scotty's mine, and who knew what he was looking for. A $60,000 grubstake was involved, so Scotty had to do something.

His friend Billy Keys had a good prospect hole, the Desert Hound Mine, which he agreed to pass off as Scotty's if the investigators got too close, but Scotty was afraid that wouldn't work. A better scheme would be to keep the Easterners away from the vicinity completely. Perhaps he could scare them off. But how? The old Buffalo Bill show came to mind. Of course—a fake holdup should do the trick.

In on Scotty's plan were his Chicago friend and benefactor Johnson, his brother Warner Scott, his crony Bill Keys, an Indian named Bob Belt, and a couple of others. In preparation for the visitors Scotty borrowed a four-mule rig and polished it up to look like what only a wealthy mining man would use for the convenience of distinguished guests. The party arrived and Scotty met them with great ceremony, introducing Johnson as a doctor in his employ at the mine. Johnson was enjoying the little joke.

The expedition was now ready for its perilous desert trek. Scotty drove the mules and as an escorting guard his brother Warner and "Doctor" Johnson rode on horseback. Scotty had warned his guests that where was grave danger in this adventure. Ruthless bandits were lurking in the hills, and the city men were risking their lives. He advised them to turn back, but they allowed as how they were willing to take the chance.

According to the plan, Keys and the Indian Belt started out a day ahead. They were to ride up the old Wingate trail and wait at the east end of Long Valley. When the Scott party reached a certain place they were to open fire and shoot one of the lead mules. Then Scotty and his helpers would quickly disconnect the dead mule, swing the team around, and race back to safety. The visitors would see that his warning had been wise, they would thank him for saving their lives, and the expedition would be called off. Buffalo Bill could not have planned it better.

But something had to go wrong. Keys and Belt reached the appointed spot and settled down behind some big rocks to wait. The Scott party was late in coming, and the wait grew tedious. It was hot, and Belt took to his canteen with increasing frequency. Keys soon learned that instead of water Belt had filled his canteen with whiskey, so they both took a drink. As time dragged on, the Indian grew more and more unsteady, and his vision began to blur. When the victims finally came within shooting distance the plan was put into operation, but somehow the shots failed to hit the mule. Belt was so drunk he couldn't aim, but one of his shots did find a target. A wild bullet struck Warner Scott in the groin.

Scotty panicked. He yelled for Belt and Keys to stop shooting. Warner would needed attention, but the fake doctor didn't know what to do. The visitors quickly saw through the trick. The expedition ended, to be sure, but the fake ambush gave the Easterners the evidence they needed to file charges against Scott. The Los Angeles newspapers made the most of the affair, and Scott had to hide out to avoid arrest. When next heard from he was in Seattle starring in a play entitled "Scotty, King of the Desert Mine."

The San Bernardino County Sheriff had warrants for the arrest of Scott, Keys, and one other suspect on charges of assault with a deadly weapon. When Scotty's show brought him back to California he was arrested but was released on bail, and the show worked its way down the state to Los Angeles. There his brother Warner surprised him with a damage suit for $152,000. But luck did not abandon him completely. It seems that the Wingate ambush had occurred in Inyo County, which had no interest in prosecuting the case. Warner finally dropped his suit, and Scotty left town. So the story of the battle of Wingate Pass was added to the Scotty legend.

Despite the Wingate fiasco, Albert Johnson continued to enjoy Scotty's company and remained loyal to him. By now, half of what Scott mined belonged to Gerard. Scott sold the other half to Johnson, who still seemed to believe that there was a real mine somewhere. He continued to grubstake his desert friend, and through 1907 Scott lived well on Johnson's money. Wherever he went he gained publicity by scattering bills where they would be most visible.

Finally, after a thorough investigation, Johnson had to face the truth: there was no mine. He cut off the flow of money, and Scott had to find a new source of income. This time it was a scam to rip off mining operators through their workers who stole chunks of ore from their diggings. Since Scotty reputedly owned a mine, he could "fence" the stolen ore for the miners and sell it legally as being from his own mine. For a time, this was a profitable enterprise.

In 1912 Scotty again created headlines for himself by announcing that he had just sold his Death Valley Gold Mine for one million dollars. The doctor who had attended Scott's brother Warner now saw his chance to collect his unpaid fee and filed a suit for the money. When Scotty refused to answer the charges he was jailed for contempt. The Grand Jury thought they possibly had a stock swindle on their hands and brought charges against Scotty.

This time there was no way out. In court Scotty had to admit that his mine in Death Valley was all a myth. In the most humiliating confession of all, Scotty had to say, "I've been a piker all my life." But this admission in open court did nothing to damage the Scotty legend. People wanted to believe in his gold mine in Death Valley and continued to do so even in the face of his denial.

In 1909 Albert Johnson returned to Death Valley. He was hooked on the place by now, as was Scotty. He knew the mine was a sham, but that didn't matter any more. He was in love with Death Valley and it took Scott to make it meaningful. He liked to go there in the wintertime for his health and to associate with this colorful desert character. He enjoyed the fantasy of living in the old wild west, and the yarns of Scotty never grew stale.

In 1922 he built a house for himself and his wife, with a small apartment in it for Scotty. He was willing and able to pay whatever it took to keep this unique man near him. Johnson had a sense of humor that made him relish the idea of keeping this other self who had dared to do the wild things that he could only dream of doing. It was here that they began to plan the enlargement of the house into something fabulous, a castle that would make the whole country take notice.

It pleased Johnson to promote the Scotty legend, keeping himself in the background to add to the air of mystery. When newsmen came in search of a feature story, he dodged their questions about himself and turned their attention to Scotty. The castle grew and so did the legend. But in 1931 the construction had to stop because Johnson had lost most of his money in the great financial crash and could no longer afford an expensive habit like Death Valley Scotty.

A couple of years later bad luck struck again. Johnson learned that because of a mistake in his deed the million dollar castle had been built on government land, not his own. It took an act of Congress to make the land available for purchase to clear his title to it. All this was expensive for Johnson, and worrisome, but Scotty consoled him with his own kind of wisdom: "You shouldn't let it get you down. That's the price you should expect to pay for being my friend."

Yet one more time Johnson's loyalty was to be tested. In 1937 Mrs. Scott sued her sometime husband for separate maintenance, and Scotty slipped from Death Valley to Arizona to avoid the process server. Johnson explained to the scandal sheet press that Scotty was broke. To fulfill a moral obligation, however, he agreed to set up a trust that would guarantee Mrs. Scott an income for life. The poor lady knew very well that the mine did not exist, but the Scotty legend had become so convincing she began to believe it herself and wanted to share in its proceeds. Despite all the evidence to the contrary, Scotty's mine refused to die, and the castle became a mecca for desert tourists.

When Johnson and his wife died, the castle was left to a religious organization, the Gospel Foundation, which ran it as a tourist attraction with Scotty in residence as the main attraction. And when he died in 1954 the national magazines and wire services recalled his famous exploits in a series of feature stories. It was long after Scotty's death, in fact in 1970, that the castle along with the rest of Johnson's holdings was purchased by the National Park Service. The Scotty legend had attained its own monument.

In an obituary notice it was said of Scotty, "His hoaxes, if they were hoaxes, his recantations, if they were recantations, provided America with entertainment. They made Scotty the man as mysterious as the wastes from which he burst forth in 1905 with his pockets full of nuggets. And one thing even the most cynical of his critics cannot dispute: showman, shyster, or just plain thief, Death Valley Scotty was undeniably an American legend, and in his own time."

SAINT PETER LISTENED to this fabulous story in silence. Not since his interview with Phineas T. Barnum had he heard such an outrageous tale. He stroked his beard and smiled a little as he thought how delighted Old Lucifer, that devious adversary of his, would be to have such a character in his infernal regions.

He tapped his fingertips gently together and considered the matter. Here was a man from California. That would normally be against him; Californians did not do well in Heaven. And yet he hadn't really hurt anybody with malice in his heart; his victims, if they were victims, had been caught by their own greed. He lived in a world of make-believe, but so did all Californians. In fact, he was the perfect embodiment of all the sins and virtues of that part of the world, a kind of archetype character. If Scotty went to Hell, all the Californians would follow, and that would upset the balance for equal opportunity in the celestial establishment.

So Death Valley Scotty got into Heaven.

Down The Hole

HE SLID OFF the roof of the little outbuilding and landed on his feet in the rubble below. Instantly the pain shot into his foot, a sharp, piercing stab, cold like a sudden shock and then hot and throbbing. He knew immediately what had happened. The nail in the board on which he had jumped must have been sticking up more than inch. His weight and the force of his fall had driven it through the rubber sole into his foot so deep that he could not pull it loose. It might have gone most of the way through the ball of his foot because he had to lean against the shed and kick the board with his other foot to pry out the nail. He felt a dull, toothache kind of pain as it came out.

He had just finished a minor repair job on the roof of a little shed behind the boarding house, a trifling favor for his landlady before going up the hill to the mine for the night shift. In fact, he was already dressed for work—heavy wool shirt and denim jumper, overalls stiffened and stained with dry mud from the work of the night before, and the buckled boots with rubber bottoms big enough to allow for the wool socks essential for warmth and comfort in the cold, wet muck of the mine.

This is stupid, he thought. He should have known better. In the three years after high school he had worked at every kind of job—

at heavy construction, at sheep shearing, on a railroad section gang, in a grocery store, and now mucking and tramming in the mine. He knew that only a fool would jump without looking.

All this experience with hard labor had been necessary to scrape up enough money to go to the university. He could not afford a senseless mistake now that would cost him even a few days' work. In a depression, four dollars a day was good pay, and he needed that money for tuition, board, and room. And with one more month of summer work he could just about make it. His first thoughts, therefore, were not of the accident or the pain of it but the possible consequences. An injury or sickness not related to the job would cost him the doctor's bill, the loss of time, and probably the loss of his job because someone else would be hired to take his place. The silver mines of Park City were not charitable, and jobs were hard to find. Fifty men would be waiting for a chance to take his place on the payroll. But if the injury had occurred in the mine, the doctor would be free and the job would be held for his return after a reasonable period of fully paid sick leave.

The pain had subsided a little, and he sat for a moment thinking. If he could get into the mine and start his shift, he could make the accident happen on the job and he would then be secure. The company would take care of everything. But that would be dishonest, and honesty was a virtue that shaped one's character. Still, the company could afford it, and he could not. The company would never know the difference if he got away with it.

But could he respect himself for stealing—for it would be like stealing—from the mine? He had never stolen anything of such a magnitude before. Would such an act diminish him and thus make him die a little? The loss of one's honor could be a kind of death. And yet his need had the force of life itself. On the other hand, even if he tried could he get away with it? It would take cunning and luck. And endurance.

Then a new thought came. He remembered that rusty nails could cause lockjaw. He had heard that people sometimes died from it. Suddenly this was a serious situation. But getting back to the

Every step was like a jab of a hot iron.

university was serious, too; it was the next step in a compelling drive to get an education, to have a career that would save him from a life of toil and poverty and frustration. The why of this single motivation was buried in details from the past that needed no remembering—how he had milked cows for his board and room during high school, how he had worked at odd jobs and saved pennies to enroll, sometimes for only one term a year because the money always ran out. These were facts from the past that merged to become an accumulation of forces to be lived with, without being analyzed. Only the total of these impressions mattered now at the surface of his consciousness. He had to get back to his education at the university.

The entrance to the mine was more than a mile away, all uphill, and to walk it would not be pleasant. Even if he got inside, how could he manage a similar accident without getting caught? He was on the night shift, which went in at four and came out at midnight. It was now three o'clock and time to get started if he intended to go at all. His dinner pail, which the landlady always packed with the same things—two sandwiches, a piece of fruit, a sweet roll or cookie, and a thermos bottle of coffee—was ready for him to pick up. His miner's cap, with its metal frontpiece for holding the carbide lamp, was waiting beside the lunch pail by the kitchen door. He tried walking and found that the sting in his injured foot was endurable. He looked at his big Picket Ben watch, slung the strap of the lunch pail over his shoulder, and called to his landlady in the house, "I guess I'll be going now."

To reach the road up to the mine he had to walk through the town. Park City was a typical mining camp, and he knew that at this hour it would be throbbing with life. The main street curved with the bottom of the canyon, and a few side streets were cut along the contours of the steep slopes on either side. Above and below the streets, hillside houses clung with one side dug into the hill and the other perched high on stilts or rock wall foundations. He always took one of these back streets to shorten the walk uphill to the mine, and on this afternoon in particular any steps he could save would be welcome. His foot was beginning to hurt in earnest now, and he wanted to get to where he could sit down as soon as possible. There was another reason to hurry; heavy storm clouds were beginning to form over the mountains to the south, and he knew the rain would soon come. A storm in the canyon might be spectacular to an observer securely sheltered, but for anyone trudging up the hill it would be an added misery. The forces of nature were not on his side this night.

Halfway to the edge of town he saw someone approaching. He soon recognized Art Koivula, a young man of Finnish descent with whom he had worked for a short time. Art was inclined to be too talkative, and under the present circumstances an encounter with him was the last thing he wanted.

"Hello," said Art. "I see you're on the night shift."

"Yeah."

"I'm on graveyard, myself, over at the Silver King. Are you still at the Alliance?"

"Yeah."

"I have the graveyard shift. Up the hill and down the hole in the middle of the night. Hell of a life. So I'm goin' down to the pool hall to kill a few hours. Say," Art continued, apparently not really expecting any response, "I've got some raffle tickets here from my mother's church. Just fifty cents, and you might win some good prizes. You interested?"

"No, I guess not. I don't have any money with me. Anyway, I never win anything. I just never am lucky." As soon as he said it, he wished he hadn't. He was standing on one foot, leaning against a stone wall on the up-side of the walk.

"Say," Art said, apparently accepting the refusal without question, "did you hear about the accident up at the King yesterday?"

"Yeah, I heard."

"Down on the nine-hundred-foot level," Art went on, "a miner on the day shift drilled into a missed hole. Blew him all to hell. I've just been up to the mortuary. Always wanted to see what a dead man looked like, especially one that's been blasted. He wasn't all laid out yet, and they showed him to me. They were still diggin' little pieces of rock out of him. Chest and half his face, just like hamburger. Down the hole's no place for nobody to work, and that's a fact. But I guess some of us ain't got no choice."

He knew well enough what Art meant. He knew about accidents and death in the mine. Earlier that summer he had helped carry out one of his partners. The man had been prying loose some overhanging rock, and a cave-in followed which buried the miner under tons of heavy jagged boulders. He had helped dig the man out. The skull was crushed, but the man remained conscious until he died just as they got him to the hospital. He remembered thinking how long the man had lived with his head open and his brains showing.

"Yeah, I guess you're right, Art," was all he could think to say at the moment. He heard thunder beyond the hills, and noticed heavy clouds forming in the canyon. "Guess I'd better be goin'," he said.

"Well, so long," said Art. "Tap 'er light. Up the hill and down the hole sure ain't no life."

The phrase "tap her light" was the miner's equivalent for "take it easy," and its use was a sign of fraternal cordiality. He liked the expression, but tonight it somehow meant a little more to him than usual, even coming from Art.

Now and then other miners heading for the same shift would come out of their yards for their long walk up the hill. Sometimes they would plod along together in little groups, but now he let them pass him. The usual greeting of "How's she goin'?" called for no particular response beyond a simple "Okay," and this time he was content to let them go on ahead so he could continue his slow walk alone.

Out of town and up the steep canyon road, two things pressed in on his consciousness—the stinging pain in his foot that was now forcing him to limp and the approaching storm. The steep canyon walls were closing in on both sides, and the darkening storm was pushing down upon him from above. He sensed that he was being caught in mighty natural forces beyond his control. He was being funneled into some black uncertain destiny where he could not see the end. But it was too late to turn back now. He plodded on, step after step, past the shops of the Daly-Judge Mine and beyond to the high gravel dump of the Alliance.

Suddenly he realized that he had no plan. How could he manage an accident in the mine that would be believable? It would have to be a situation that could explain stepping on a nail, but there were no boards with nails in them lying around in the tunnel where he worked. He was one of a team of three working in the "face" of a "drift," or minor tunnel. He was the trammer, whose job it was to push the loaded cars out to the hoist; there was a mucker who loaded the cars, and the third was the miner, who set up his drill, put in the holes, packed them with dynamite sticks, and set them off at the end of the shift. The shift boss, or "shifter," would come around once during the night to see if everything was going properly, and it was to him that an accident has to be reported.

He remembered that not far back from the face of the tunnel there was a small drift that extended about thirty yards off from the tunnel at right angles. It had not led to any ore, so it was abandoned, and in it was a small pile of trash—bits of broken hose, some pieces of useless track, and a few empty powder boxes. These were the wooden crates that the sticks of dynamite came in, and they were held together with nails. If the rubbish had not been cleaned out and the broken boxes carried away, he might pull it off. This might work if he could tell a good story and if the shift boss believed it. Anyway, it was the only plan he could think of.

The rain was beginning to fall as he limped around the shop at the mine entrance and took shelter under the long shed where the cars of the man-train would soon come to take the workers into the mine. Some twenty-five or thirty men had already gathered, waiting for the long ride through the main tunnel to the station inside, from whence they would disperse to their various work places on the several levels of the mine. As he sat down and stretched his leg out to ease the throbbing foot, one of the men noticed his limp.

"Looks like you got a sore foot, there," the man remarked with only mild interest.

"Yeah. Got an ingrown toenail, that's all," he answered. The man grunted. There was other conversation going on that was much more interesting. Some of the men were savoring a new yarn about one Patrick Sullivan, better known as Paddy-the-Pig, a gigantic and colorful tramp miner with a reputation for fabulous fights and equally exaggerated red-light district exploits that spread from Butte to Arizona and all the mining camps between.

They could hear the train coming that would bring out the day shift and take them aboard for its return trip down the hole, and the waiting miners stirred to life. He hobbled over to the keg of carbide that supplied them with fuel for their lamps, took out his Prince Albert smoking tobacco can and scooped it full of the foul-smelling granules, loaded the fuel chamber of his cap lamp, and shoved the tobacco can back into his pocket. This was the final ritual that indicated the men were ready for the darkness below. Now it meant his last chance to change his mind and turn back. He felt that his foot had grown tighter in his boot. It was probably swelling. He remembered again some of the reports he had heard about getting lockjaw from rusty nails. Or possibly an infection and blood poisoning. He had had a bad case of blood poisoning once— got it from a tick bite that had festered in his hand. Were some people more susceptible to blood poisoning than others? He didn't know.

The work train backed to a stop under the long shed at the mouth of the mine, and the men began to climb aboard. The motor was a low-built boxlike trolley with a pole that reached up to the bare electric wire overhead and the motorman sat in a small seat like a cockpit safely situated below the trolley wheel. The cars that carried the workmen were flat, with a kind of bench lengthwise down the center. The men straddled it, five or six to a car, for the long ride through the tunnel to the hoist station inside. The tunnel was over a mile long into the very heart of the mountain, and except for the occasional faint reflection of the motor's headlight it was a curving artery of total blackness. The little train gained speed, and into the deep caves of the earth they went.

He usually enjoyed the ride into the mine. The clickety-click, clickety-click, clickety-click of the wheels on the rails seemed like a rhythmic beating of life defying the black caverns of death. It reminded him of how Dante must have felt, listening for some reassuring sound of life, as Virgil led him into the silent bowels of hell. But this time it was different. He was being sucked deeper and deeper into a blind unknown. He was no longer in control of his ultimate destiny. Now he would have to play out the hand that fate was dealing.

They reached the station, a vast well-lighted cavern comfortably dry and warm from the machinery that chugged and whirred with the inner life of the mine—compressors that pumped air through a network of tubes to feed power to the jackhammers and liner drills at the end of every tunnel, drift, or stop where holes were to be drilled for the blasting; and the giant hoist with its hundreds of feet of cable that pulled the cage and its loads of men, equipment, ore, and waste up and down the shaft. The station was on the five-hundred-foot level at the end of the main tunnel. When the miners dispersed to their various working areas they were hoisted up to the two-hundred level or dropped to the seven-hundred, nine-hundred, or twelve-hundred foot levels. Each crew of miners knew where to go and what to do when they got there unless the shift boss changed their assignment. Usually no questions were asked and conversation was sparse, except for a few ribald jibes at certain good natured characters with a reputation for romancing, fighting, or drinking. He and his two partners got into the cage and were lowered to the seven-hundred level. They greeted each other casually, as usual. There were no close bonds of friendship in the mine; men came and went without surprise or personal concern on either side. What each man did on the outside was his own business. There was one exception to this tacit rule, however; whenever there was danger, great or small, every miner would spring to the aid of his companion. Like soldiers in battle, they looked after each other with all the strength they had or all the tender care and compassion that was called for. That was why he could not let his limp be detected as they walked from the hoist platform into their tunnel. Being the trammer he, as usual, pushed an empty car before him and he could lean against it to ease the weight on his throbbing foot.

"I wonder how big the muckpile will be this time," said the mucker. He always said that, always hoping that it would not be too big to shovel into the cars in a single shift. A mucker was in disgrace if he failed to clean up the pile during his shift, for the mucker on the next shift would have that much more rock to move.

Their tunnel—or drift, actually, which was smaller than a tunnel and was cut as an exploratory thrust toward what was hoped to be a vein or lode of silver, lead, and zinc—was a long tube of total blackness. The little flame from their head lamps on their caps, with the metal reflector behind it, gave them enough light. Halfway in, they passed the small lateral drift into which the old powder boxes had been thrown. He paused long enough to cast his beam of light into the drift to see whether the pile of rubbish had been cleaned out. Without the nails in those broken boxes, he would have no possible way of simulating his accident. The trash was still there.

They continued on to the face of the drift where their work lay. On the night shift they would be alone; the timbermen and the trackmen worked only on the day shift, so no one else would be working there. The boss always made his rounds, but it would be two or three hours before he put in his appearance. Until then the work had to proceed as usual.

The muck pile from the previous shift's blasting was not too large, and everything else was as it should be. Air was hissing out of the half-open valve in the compressed air pipeline, and the miner turned it off; every workshift left the air open to clear out the smoke from the blast. The miner and mucker then began to "bar down" the ceiling and sides to pry loose any insecure rock debris that might fall on them while they worked, and then they set about the two-man job of screwing into place the heavy iron bar that would hold the liner drilling machine. While this was going on, a second empty car had to be brought in from the hoist landing so the mucker could always be shoveling the rock into one while the other was being trammed out.

He was in real pain now. Every step was like the jab of a hot iron. He hoped the boss would come soon so he could report his accident and get out of there. The shift boss—now, here was a new problem. The boss was an angular, awkward man named Baxter, with an ugly scar sloping from the side of his mouth to his chin. He didn't like Baxter, and he was pretty sure that Baxter didn't like him. For one thing, it had become known that his urge to get back to the university was so he could continue his pre-law course and eventually become an attorney. Unfortunately, Baxter, now in middle age, had been frustrated in his own desire to get an education and had come to envy and hate the younger men who were working their way toward a better life outside the mine.

Now his fear was that Baxter would try to cross-examine him about his accident. The success or failure of his scheme depended on whether the boss would accept his story and give him sick leave. He knew that Baxter would not hesitate to condemn him if he got the chance. There could be no slip-up. On his way back with an empty car he stopped at the side drift and went back to its face to examine the old powder boxes. They had nails in them, but they were small, much smaller than the one that had pierced his foot. This would have to do, however, and he moved the boards around so several of the nails were sticking up.

Back at the face, the miner was drilling his holes and the mucker was filling his car. To ease the foot he sat down, hoping the boss would not be too long in coming. A light showed in the drift, and he knew the time had come; Baxter would be there in a minute. He began to swear, loud enough for the boss to hear him. In the mine, whenever anything went wrong, the man who could swear the hardest was the least likely to be blamed. Some of them had developed a ritualistic flow of profanities and obscenities that excelled in eloquence, an art that he had learned well enough.

Baxter came close and beamed the light into his face. "What's the matter with you?" he asked. With appropriate expletives the prepared story was told.

"What the hell were you doing back in that drift?" Baxter wanted to know.

"I went back there to take a leak."

The miner had stopped drilling, and the mucker had paused in his shoveling to listen. This was a surprising development that might concern them. The boss, without a word, turned and went back to examine the side drift.

"Hurt much?" the miner asked with genuine sympathy.

"Yeah. Hurts like hell," he answered.

In a few minutes Baxter returned. "You think you can finish the shift?" he asked.

"No, I don't think so. It's starting to hurt pretty bad. I wouldn't want it to turn to blood poisoning on me."

The boss looked at the muck pile. It was about half gone already, and the remainder could be shoveled out without undue effort. He turned to the mucker.

"Do you think you could tram this stuff out if I let this knuckle-headed punk go down the hill?"

"Oh, sure, I can do 'er." The mucker knew that anyone in the mine would do the same for him if the need arose.

"Well, then, you go on up to the station. I'll be along in about an hour and give you a ticket to the doctor," Baxter grunted. As he walked away into the darkness he mumbled, half to himself, "We'll have to get that damn junk pile out of that drift."

The foot was no better, but at least it was no worse. Out at the hoist platform he pulled the rope that gave the hoistman the signal to lower and then raise the cage to the station above. In the warmth of the station he rested until Baxter appeared and gave him the necessary piece of paper. No words were spoken, but he fancied that Baxter gave him a long, searching look that meant suspicion, and he wondered if questions might be asked later. When the ore train was ready for the long trip to the outside, he climbed aboard.

It was still raining when he started his walk down the canyon to the town below. Night was a bad time to be in trouble; he knew that no doctor would be available until morning; he had to get home and then wait.

Going down the hill was slow torture. Soaking wet and dragging his leg like an old man with a disabling stroke, he finally reached his little room at the boarding house. When he removed the boot he found that his foot was red and swollen. There was nothing he could do for it now but go to bed and try to rest. But he couldn't sleep. His thoughts were on tomorrow.

He was up before anyone was stirring in the house. His foot was too big for his shoe and too tender for any pressure, so with one shoe on and a heavy sock on the bad foot he limped the three blocks down to the main street where the company doctor had his office. The rain had stopped. It would be a clear warm morning.

The town was not yet fully awake. The doctor's office was a front room at the street level of an old hotel, but the door was locked and no one was stirring about the place. He sat down on the porch and waited, not knowing how long it would be before the doctor showed up.

The town gradually awakened. A newsboy zoomed by on a motorcycle—the hills were too steep for bicycles—and the morning paper was tossed onto the porch of the hotel. A small truck rattled past, loaded with bottles of milk destined for doorways further down the canyon. The pool hall next door, with its gambling tables in the back room and probably a good supply of bootleg liquor under the "soft drink" bar, was locked and silent; it would not open until noon.

He waited, hoping the doctor would come early, but he knew better; the doctor would probably go, first to the hospital, which was some distance out of town, before coming to the office. At about eight-thirty the miners from the graveyard shift drifted into town, most of them heading for their boarding houses scattered

along the main street. A few of the men had families living in small
houses on the streets below town, and he watched them walk by.
Now and then an old car loaded with workmen would come along.
Most of the miners were drifters whose lives were spent a third of
the time underground, a third sleeping, and the rest of the time in
the boarding house or pool hall playing cards or getting drunk. But
there were those, too, who raised their families and lived out their
lives in the town, and sometimes they could afford an automobile,
even in a mountain town with steep rocky streets that were hard on
cars.

He watched the town come to life, and waited. Finally, after
several hours, the doctor arrived. He followed the doctor into the
office and produced the precious piece of paper the shift boss had
given him. He told his story, and the doctor looked at the foot.

"Have you had a tetanus shot?" the doctor asked.

No, he had never had one. So the doctor quickly took care of that
detail.

"We'll have to get you to the hospital as soon as possible," the
doctor said. "I'll take you in my car right now."

Most of the patients at the hospital were miners, although the
townspeople who could not afford to go to the city for treatment
came there also. It was a big two-story mansion converted to
medical purposes, which served very well for care and treatment of
the patients of the two doctors in the town. Two nurses, with other
incidental help, kept the place running. They were efficient and
cheerful, when they were not being bossy, and he felt comfortable
with the whole situation. The burden had been shifted from his
shoulders, and he could relax. His fate was no longer in jeopardy,
and that was a relief.

The doctor's orders were to soak the foot in a hot ten percent
Lysol solution for two hours at a time for the first couple of days,
and that should take care of the problem. So he sat with his foot in
a pan of hot water watching his foot shrivel down to a normal size,
puckered and wrinkled from the treatment.

Now he had time to think about other things. His plans were

back on track again. Looking back on the pain and fear of the night before, he wondered if there was any lesson to be learned from all this. He would return to his job without any loss in pay, and he could get back to the university for the next term. Did this mean that crime pays after all? Or did it mean that persistence, endurance, and a little pain must put one to the test if he is to succeed in life? Or could it mean, as he had once heard a psychology professor say, that our fears are mostly of dangers created in the mind and what seems like dire necessity or ghosts are but specters of the mind? He didn't know. Maybe it didn't matter so much after all. The pretty, young nurse's aide was coming to sit and visit with him, and this was no time for heavy thinking.

The Celebrated Millard County
Dramatic Stock Company

IT WAS A MARVELOUS YEAR, 1927. Charles Lindbergh made his epic flight to Paris, penicillin was discovered to have antibiotic properties, B. Traven wrote *The Treasure of the Sierra Madre,* and Al Jolson starred in the first talking picture, *The Jazz Singer.* And also the prodigious and memorable dramatic stock company of Millard County, Utah, was born. It was more specifically advertised as "The Frank Rasmussen Players" for the obvious reason that the founder of this troupe of actors was the locally esteemed Frank Rasmussen, who directed, produced and acted in the plays and collected the gate receipts whenever there happened to be any. The surrogate mother of this family of theatrical dreamers was the Millard County High School, which delivered up to the world a few graduates who were aspiring thespians inspired by their speech and drama teacher, Mr. Rasmussen.

Up to that time the town of Fillmore had produced only two or three illustrious people with reputations that reached beyond the county line, and one of these was Mr. Rasmussen, who had left home as a young man to join a traveling tent show company. He had made a meager but obviously respectable living playing small roles in various theatrical enterprises "back east," and at the pinnacle of his career he had even taken a bit part in a Hollywood movie. With this reputation he was welcomed home to Fillmore and given a teaching job in the local high school, where he produced plays for the delight and entertainment of the local populace.

When the summer of 1927 dawned and the high school seniors were duly graduated, and some of them were thinking of careers that would take them out into the world, it was Mr. Rasmussen who came up with the great idea. He gathered together some of his more talented disciples, I among them, and with the chivalrous gleam of knighthood in his eye—or perhaps more like Moses returning from Sinai with the tablets—he proclaimed: "I have here a play. It's a good comedy and audiences will love it. I call it *Turn to the Right* because it has a happy ending, but that's not its real title; if we used the real title we would have to pay royalties to the company that published the original. There's a part in it for each of you. You will gain some valuable experience in the theatre, and— Who knows?—you might go on to find a glorious career in acting. There won't be any money in it, but if you don't have anything better to do this summer you will find it very interesting to live the lives of traveling players."

We didn't have anything better to do, and we found his idea very interesting indeed. We had a reading of the play, Mr. Rasmussen assigned us roles which we were confident we could play with conviction and dramatic enthusiasm, and rehearsals began. Lillian Littledyke was to be the leading lady, a fragile blonde innocent type who ultimately triumphed in romance with the tall, handsome leading man, who was Orlondo Huntsman. Incidentally, that was genuine type casting; he played that role in real life as a high school student as well. Ruth Scottern was the poor widowed mother, and a couple of other girls had supporting roles.

Mr. Rasmussen and Everett Ashman were dastardly gangsters who were hiding out in the small town where the dramatic action took place; their function in the play was to plot and scheme and cheat the widowed mother and in general create suspense and plot entanglements. I was the comic, a country bumpkin really smarter than he seemed, who became rich in the third act for making and selling strawberry jam made from his mother's secret recipe. Also joining the cast was Dr. Baker, Fillmore's local physician, who thought he had a talent for acting and wanted some diversion from his not-too-demanding practice.

Most of us had other responsibilities in addition to our roles in the play. Ruth Scottern was to collect the money, pay the bills, and keep track of whatever business details might arise. Byron Ray handled publicity in the country's weekly newspaper and attended to the printing of programs and distribution of posters announcing our coming. I was to be the stage manager, and Mr. Rasmussen, of course, was the director. All in all, as well as being gifted and ambitious actors, we were a well organized dramatic company. No one could yet say for sure, but it was possible that with a start like this we might wind up playing in a Salt Lake City theatre, or even in New York. The more we talked about it the higher our aspirations soared. All we needed was a good start and a few lucky breaks. Byron even offered—if it would help the show, that is—to do some tricks of magic between the acts just to keep the audience amused, but Mr. Rasmussen didn't think that would be necessary.

Like a good Broadway show that always opened out of town, we decided to test the play as well as the audience—and incidentally make sure that we knew our lines—in the town of Scipio, which was a rural metropolis of about four hundred residents. It was a farming village so isolated it didn't even have a movie theatre. We reasoned that the good citizens of Scipio must surely be hungry for genuine professional drama. Accordingly, the date was set and posters were put in the window of the one store and on a tree near the front of the church.

On the appointed day we arrived in the afternoon to set up the props and make sure there were lights for the stage and seats for the audience. The town marshal, who was also the janitor, let us into the ancient hall. Its stage was small and there was no scenery, but we thought we could adapt to those minor defects. The place was dirty and unkempt from obvious long disuse. "Ain't held nothin' in here since the new church was built, goin' on two, three years, I guess," the marshal explained. "I'll see that the chairs are all set up for you, and I guess you can manage with what goes on the stage."

We set to work clearing out some debris that had accumulated on what passed for a stage. Not so bad, we thought, for a small town. We set up some scenery, arranged props, and found a table to put in the small adjacent room that would serve as a dressing room for the girls. It had a pile of boards and boxes in one corner, but finding no other place for them we just left the mess there. We grew more tense as curtain time approached. A few people were beginning to filter in and take seats. Every now and then one of us would peek through a hole in the curtain to see how the audience was growing. The girls were in their dressing room putting on costumes, and Mr. Rasmussen was inspecting the set to make sure everything was ready.

Then it happened. If George Washington's boat had capsized and sunk half way across the Delaware, he would not have been in a more critical situation than we were. A wild scream suddenly pierced the silence of the dressing room, and the girls came running out. With them emerged the most nauseating odor which, being country folk, we recognized immediately. One of the girls had moved some of the boxes in the dressing room corner and roused a skunk that had been nesting there. Out came the girls, out came the skunk, and out came the sharp, penetrating odor. Someone opened the back door, and the terrified animal escaped. But the smell remained. It saturated the back stage area and quickly spread out into the audience.

"Happens ever' now and again," the marshal explained. "Smells pretty bad, don't it?" Pretty bad? It was unendurable. A couple of the more heroic members of our cast rushed into the dressing room, grabbed the trash on which the acrid elixir had been deposited, and threw it out into the back yard. Doors and windows were frantically opened for ventilation, and the audience, which had grown to about forty people, began to squirm.

What were we to do now? Cancel the performance? But the show must go on, we had been taught. Give the audience back their money? But we needed that money to pay expenses. Would the career of our dramatic stock company end in disaster before it began? Surely God could not be so cruel. Speaking for God on this occasion, the marshal calmly gave his opinion. "I think you can go on with your show. We'll just air the place out a little and give it time to blow out. Folks around here are used to things like that." As if taking a silent cue from God, several men rose from the audience and opened all the doors and windows, and a few women fanned the air with shawls and aprons.

Our manager, the redoubtable Mr. Rasmussen, like a veteran sea captain who had weathered many a storm, went forth to placate the audience. "Ladies and Gentlemen," he said in his most resonant theatrical voice, "as you know by now we have encountered some unexpected difficulties back stage. I can now assure you that the problem has been solved and the matter has been cleared up—or will be cleared up shortly—so if you will bear with us a little while longer the show will go on as scheduled. We thank you."

The show did go on, though somewhat tainted. By the time we got to the third and final act, we were beginning to feel that our disaster had been averted and we were saved. Our hopes soared up again like fire. That night, on our way back to our home base in Fillmore, we began to feel good about the experience. We hadn't made any money, but at least we were once again on the threshold of a possible career as a dramatic stock company. Tomorrow night we would play in Fillmore to a big audience in Bartholomew Hall. We knew our lines and had had our dress rehearsal. Byron summed it up for all of us. "At least, you can say we made a big stink in Scipio," he said.

So the next night in Fillmore we were at a high pitch of excitement, ready to give a perfect performance and win applause from an appreciative audience, most of whom would know us personally and expect only the best. Of course, Dr. Baker had to spend the day at his office attending to his practice, and Mr. Rasmussen had to help his brother repair a chicken coop, but the rest of us were diligently making ready. Mr. Bartholomew had reason to be proud of his new establishment. It was a combination of dance hall and roller skating rink, with an ample stage for dramatic productions. When chairs were arranged on the dance floor it became a large auditorium, just the place for our thespian triumph.

As show time approached we were delighted to see, through our peephole in the curtain, that a large audience had assembled. At fifty cents a head, the gate receipts would be gratifying, and we would be on our way to fortune and fame. The play moved along beautifully, and our spirits continued to rise. The audience laughed, and everything was going well. That is, until the middle of the second act.

I was not on stage for the scene that was playing; that was when Dr. Baker in his role, and Ruth Scottern playing the poor widowed mother, were doing something in a sweet and tender part of the plot. The audience sat still and attentive, listening to every word. Just at that enchanting moment a wild man burst through the door and ran toward the stage shouting, "Doctor Baker! Is Doctor Baker here? I want Doctor Baker! My wife is having a baby, and the doctor has to come right now!"

The scene came to an abrupt and confusing end, and Dr. Baker slipped away with the frantic husband leaving us to finish the play as best we could. But we remembered that the show must go on. There was no one in the cast who could finish the doctor's role, and two more scenes called for his presence. Luckily Mr. Rasmussen's brother Will was in the audience. I went down and got him to come back stage, and we thrust a script into his trembling hand. At the right time we pushed him out on stage and he read the lines of the missing doctor. The scenes went on and the audience accepted the situation as part of the comedy. The play ended with God in His heaven and all right with the world. Except that Dr. Baker did not return to the cast. He decided that his patients came first, and acting was not his forte. But that wasn't too great a loss for us; we persuaded brother Will that he was the legitimate understudy, and he took over the doctor's part. And Byron said, "That's a good sign. We've had a production and a reproduction on the same night."

But our optimism was premature. The next night in the little town of Meadow Creek the crisis that befell us was more serious than either a skunk or a baby—if those two miracles of nature can appropriately be mentioned in the same breath. We had a good audience, people were laughing, and the play was going well. I was on stage involved in some funny business with Byron and a couple of the other characters. Mr. Rasmussen, who was behind the scenes, could not see the disaster and didn't know what was happening, but I was where I could witness it all. Suddenly and without warning a man sitting on about the sixth row fell out of his chair, lurched forward, and crumpled on the floor. Everyone turned to look, and several people near him sprang out of their seats and crouched around him to administer what aid they could.

Our scene stopped dead. We could only stand there and watch as the whole audience squirmed and peered at the man on the floor. My first thought was that the man had died of a heart attack. He would be the close friend of everybody in town, and our audience would leave. This would be the end of our performance. What were we to do? At the moment, all we could do was freeze in our places and watch. Mr. Rasmussen stuck his head through the scenery and in a frantic stage whisper hissed, "What happened? What's wrong?"

On stage we could only pretend not to hear. Of all nights, this was the one when Dr. Baker should have been with us. The death of a man in the audience would kill our play as well. What happened next was like a movie scene cut to slow motion. Several men picked up the limp, convulsing figure and carried him forward to the foot of the stage. We could see the victim's distorted face. From the side of my mouth I whispered to Byron, "Is he dead?"

"Looks dead to me," Byron answered as he leaned forward to get a better look.

The men carried the poor fellow across to a side door near the stage and disappeared into the hallway beyond. We waited. Gradually the other people in the audience began to take their seats again and turn their attention to the stage. We still waited, not knowing what to do next. Then the men who had removed the victim returned to their places and sat down. So we went on and played the scene, which fortunately ended the act.

The moment the curtain closed, we rushed off stage amidst confusion and dismay. Someone was sent out to learn what had happened. When he came back the janitor was with him. "You don't need to worry none," he reassured us. "The feller's an epileptic, and sometimes he takes a fit. Folks around here know all about it. He'll be all right again pretty soon, so don't worry. Just go on with your show." So we did go on and finish the play, but some of us were beginning to have doubts about the unqualified pleasure in a career with a traveling dramatic stock company.

That night Byron made us feel a little better about it. "We sure knocked 'em dead in Meadow Creek," he quipped. "Really had 'em rolling in the aisles, didn't we?"

Our next engagement was in the town of Beaver. We were scheduled to perform in a big hall that the locals called their opera house. The chairs for the audience had been placed about a hundred yards back from the vast empty stage. We could make do without scenery, but we dreaded the prospect of shouting such a distance to reach the audience. That is, if there was to be an audience. Byron and Mr. Rasmussen drove around the center of town and could not find any of the posters we had sent ahead to announce our coming, not in a store window or even on a post or tree.

"What became of our advertising posters?" Mr. Rasmussen wanted to know when the sexton arrived to light up the place.

"Oh, I didn't put 'em up in town. Last Sunday was Decoration Day, and I took 'em all out to the cemetery where I thought people would see 'em."

Apparently the people who saw our notices mistook them for obituaries. About a dozen people showed up to watch our performance, and we played that night to a hundred empty chairs. Some of the troupe argued for canceling the engagement, but Mr. Rasmussen reminded us that the show must go on. He didn't say on what. A few of us, however, were once again beginning to have doubts about show business as a career. What we needed, of course, was a renewal of faith. And it was Mr. Rasmussen's mission to restore our hope and make us born-again acolytes in the sacred rites of Thespis. In short, he concluded that we should give the theatre one more chance.

At least, Byron's hopes were revived. "We just might make a go of it," he said in a half-musing voice that seemed to come out of the future. "Some of us, anyway."

"How could that be?" I asked, probing the unknown.

"Well, what if there was a talent scout from Hollywood in the audience some time? He would see one or two of us and then we'd get invited to take a screen test. That does happen, you know. Then what if we got to be movie stars? Of course we'd have to change our names, then."

"Well, I'm not sure about being a movie star," I countered.

"Stranger things have happened."

"But if you did get to be a movie star, why change your name?"

"Everybody in the movies has a different name. You know that."

"Maybe so. If you were to be discovered and go to Hollywood and get to be a movie star, what name would you want to choose for yourself?"

"Oh, I don't know. But it would have to be something special. Like—well, maybe something like Whitney Cumberland."

"Whitney Cumberland! What kind of name is that?"

"That could be my stage name."

"We'll keep it in mind," I said.

Our next performance was scheduled to be in Milford, where we could expect a different kind of audience. Milford was a railroad town, and we would have people who had seen dramatic productions in the big cities. If they liked our show, that would prove that we had something good going for us after all.

Fortunately we did have a good audience in Milford. They laughed at the funny stuff and even at things we didn't expect to be funny. All went well until we were taking our places for the curtain to rise for the last act. The curtain was one of those big heavy things with a landscape or Greek temple or some such scene painted on the outside. It rolled up from the bottom, wrapping itself around a long pole that was operated from a pulley at the top. You could raise the curtain by pulling the rope, and when it reached the proper height you would tie the rope to a peg and thus hold it in place. To bring it down you simply released the rope and let it fall as slowly as you wished. The sexton was on hand to raise and lower the curtain on cue from one of us.

At the beginning of the last act we were all supposed to be on stage having some kind of social gathering. As the country bumpkin I had made my fortune in strawberry jam and was giving a party. The two con men were about to be foiled and ultimately reformed. Sweet young Lillian and her hero Orlondo were becoming reconciled for their happy-ever-after romance, and the poor widowed mother had her mortgage back and was almost free from whatever other jeopardy she was in. The play was heading for its final happy ending, and we were all in our places.

The sexton was in place, too. Right on cue he began to pull on his rope. The demure Lillian, alas, was standing too close to the curtain. As it rolled up, her dress caught in the winding scroll. Higher went the curtain, and her dress slowly rolled up with it. She let out a piercing shriek and began to dance from one foot to the other, but the sexton kept on pulling. The skirts went higher and higher, revealing parts of Lillian that should have remained covered. The audience roared with laughter and applauded wildly. When the bewildered sexton finally saw what was happening he let go the rope altogether and the curtain dropped, hitting the stage with a heavy thud. At that same instant poor Lillian had one foot in the wrong place, and the pole on which the curtain was rolled fell on her toes. There was another scream and the difference between comedy and tragedy became a bit indistinct.

We did finish the play. The audience loved it, but for reasons not too flattering to our artistic talents. Our sweet Lillian swore with an unprintable oath that she would never set foot on a stage again. Byron said, "I think I'll go to the university and become a doctor." We were all glad to leave Milford that night.

I went with Byron to seek another career. Whitney Cumberland was never born. Mr. Rasmussen went back to Fillmore and finished repairing his brother's chicken coop, and the celebrated Millard County dramatic stock company, better known as "The Frank Rasmussen Players," faded into memory.

Going Home

"WHAT WAS HIS NAME, NOW? You know, the fellow from Boston? He was with us for awhile at Ma Canfield's boarding house. He had some bad luck, as I remember, but I don't recall his name."

His name was Arthur Hemphill. But that was when he was alive. When a man is dead it doesn't really matter what his name was. When a man is dead he is no longer a person. Merely dust. There were times when he thought: So what's the difference? I might as well be dead. One of the walking dead. I am not really a Hemphill any more. Where I am now there is no one to put his hand on my shoulder and call me Arthur. I am no different now from thousands of others who have melted like ghosts into some anonymous herd of humanity trudging silently on toward a dark and unknown destiny.

Maybe it didn't matter much after all, he thought, that he was no different from all those others who had become nameless, faceless, homeless castaways like so much human flotsam set adrift by the crash of 1929 and the depression that followed. It was better not to think too long on what or who he had been when he was alive—a successful and prosperous man dealing in stocks and bonds, a citizen of Boston with a wife and two children—when he was the

126

respected Arthur Hemphill. Better not to dwell too much on himself and his own troubles, but he couldn't help thinking over and over again, and at the oddest moments, about the kids and their hopes and dreams. He could not put aside the thoughts about his wife—beautiful girl, strong and gifted woman, passionate lover, devoted mother, dear companion, and sharer of those years of work and play, joys and disappointments.Perhaps he should not try to retain any memories of his family back in Boston. And yet such thoughts gave him a flash of courage and perhaps a little hope. He wanted somehow to get home again.

He had come west to find a job. There was no place in Boston for a man who had been respectably high up in a brokerage firm that had disintegrated in the crash. No jobs of any kind—only long lines of bewildered men looking for work. In Chicago, lines of men in sun-faded hats or sagging caps and frayed trousers, waiting for a soup kitchen to open. In Denver, lines of men with hollow faces, silently standing. In Los Angeles the same men, still waiting. President Hoover had said that prosperity was just around the corner. But what corner? Where was the corner? There are two sides to a corner, the inside and the outside. A corner is a trap. If you are on the outside you can turn and go another direction, but if you are on the inside you can be caught by high walls of time and space and circumstance. So Hoover was wrong, he thought. A corner can stop you cold. This was 1932 and he was cold. Los Angeles was cold, and he was thinking of home.

An old friend from the good years and now living in Los Angeles had made him welcome as a guest. As a guest? More like a freeloader, he thought, who had already worn out his welcome. For more than a month, now, he had been a guest, had borrowed small change for carfare, and had increased the friend's grocery bill. He had to find work, and soon. This was the end of the line. Every day he walked from where the streetcar had dropped him on Wilshire Boulevard; he plodded for miles westward, or north, or south. A grocery store: Do you need any help today? Well, thanks, anyway. A corner fruit stand: Would you have a job, perhaps on the night

shift? Well, thanks; sorry to bother you. A Woolworth store: I
thought you might need a janitor. Well, then, maybe a stock clerk?
No, I didn't think you would need experience to handle crates or
keep the stock in order. At a cafeteria on a dirty side-street not far
from the financial district: Maybe you need a dishwasher today?
Not even for a free lunch? Yes, things are tough all over.

Day after day the same routine. Your shoes wear thin spots in
the soles. Your legs get tired and your stomach grows flat. You sit
down to rest on the stone bench in front of the city library. The
wind toys with a few dead leaves, whirling and skipping them
around in aimless eddies until it tires of the game and drops them
in some lifeless corner against the curb. People walk by, but they
don't see you. Long ago the fellow on the stage had said, "To be or
not to be, that is the question." But is it really the question? In not
being, would the pain cease? Would it be only selfishness to blot out
the hope that your loved ones still cling to, so far away? Is there
something yet to be found just around the corner? Arthur
Hemphill was tired. He wanted to go home.

The truck driver that picked him up in San Bernardino wanted
to talk. How far you going? To Salt Lake. Got a job there? No, but
I have a kind of second cousin there who runs a boarding house. I'll
be all right there for a little while until I can get on my feet and
raise enough money to get home on. Yes, I can drive. And he
thought, you can catch a little sleep that way. There isn't much
traffic on the highway this time of night, and I'll be glad to do what
I can to earn my way. This was in his mind, but he didn't say it.

Anna Canfield was his remote cousin in Salt Lake, whom he had
known only slightly years before. She and her husband had opened
their home to borders because the money came in handy—when it
came in at all. Some of the borders were none too regular with their
payments, and occasionally one would disappear owing more than
he could pay. The five or six young men who were steady and
dependable ate and slept there, came and went, developed informal
friendships, and diplomatically complimented or privately joked
about Ma and Pa Canfield. Some were students from country towns

in Idaho or remote parts of Utah whose parents had the money to support them while attending a nearby business college, a somewhat doubtful endeavor since most of them would ultimately return to the country and become farmers.

One regular member of the household was a typesetter who was always able to find a job that paid good money even in the depression, but his addiction to gambling kept him broke. He looked rather too much like the long-chinned thin man in Toulouse-Lautrec's posters for the Moulin Rouge. That could have been why his romantic pursuits—a subject of constant conversation and boasting among the other borders—always ended in failure for him. Apparently the gambling gave him a sense of importance; a man with money commanded respect, and one who could risk it with cavalier recklessness and lose it with stoic dignity was to be admired.

Another younger lodger cynically joked about having three legs—two crutches and one good limb, the other having been withered in his infancy by polio. He was shy around strangers, and among friends was easily offended. In the glib bantering boarding-house talk around him he listened, not for what was actually being said, but for what might be meant between the lines to demean him.

The boarders all paid one dollar a day for their keep, but Mr. Hemphill—because he was a middle-aged business man who had been very successful in Boston and had a good education and was a source of pride to the Canfield family for his success and genteel elegance—was welcomed with awe into the boarding house clan as an honored guest. He brought an air of dignity to the dinner-table conversation.

He played his role modestly enough as the affluent stock broker temporarily embarrassed by the depression but a symbol of hope for the students and a fatherly conscience for the typesetter. Ma Canfield bragged about him to the boarders. She also praised the printer because he always paid his rent on time, a tactic which encouraged the gambler to settle up with her before he lost his money at the illegal card table downtown. She boasted about the lad on crutches for his courage in facing the world with his handicap, and he stood a little taller for it. She also bragged about her cooking, even though she was probably the poorest cook that ever ran a boarding house. If she particularly praised a casserole or stew she was about to serve them, the boarders knew the meal would be exceptionally bad, but they always ate it with pretended appreciation. Her displeasure was to be avoided, and he who stirred her to wrath could find himself looking for another place to live. To put it simply, her boarders were all intimidated. So when she announced as a fact that Mr. Hemphill would soon be on his feet again, no one dared to doubt it, not even Mr. Hemphill.

Pa Canfield, on the other hand, did not dominate anybody. He was a small man, quick in speech and movement, witty at times, with language that was direct and unadorned; when he did express his views—which he had learned not to do in the presence of his wife—they were realistic and forthright. To him the ungainly printer was likeable enough personally, but an incurable gambler who lacked the strength of character to save himself, a man to be pitied but not praised. To him the frustrated lad on crutches had to do better in his business college courses than everybody else to succeed in life, and it was not yet apparent that he was working as hard as he should in school. And to him Mr. Hemphill was a tragic case, a man once great among his kind, who had fallen into misfortune through no fault of his own and had lost his spirit. A whipped dog always cringes, even after he has run away from a cruel master. But Pa Canfield kept such thoughts to himself. His daily routine was fixed and comfortable. After attending to his habitual morning chores he would disappear for the afternoon to play a card game called "slough" for pleasure, not gambling, with a few select cronies downtown. Then at four o'clock he would go to his job on the night shift at the railroad station where he checked baggage until midnight. With such a schedule he was never in conflict with anyone.

Arthur Hemphill fitted into this household, first with embarrassment because he could not pay his way, and then gradually with ease and contentment. He would pay later when he found a way to make money again. Ma Canfield's constant flattery helped him to regain some self-respect. He would find a job sooner or later and then go back to Boston and rescue his family from the relatives with whom they had been living. He wrote letters to them, and for the first time in months he signaled the hope that he would find his way home again.

The leaves of the calendar turned over, and it was December. Cold winds swept in from the western desert, and the winter rain peppered against the windows. Out in the country the cattle huddled together with their backs to the storm, and the tumbleweeds, now dead and crisp and brown, were torn loose from their shallow roots and rolled by the wind to pile up in the fence corners where they would lodge until the decaying process of nature would reduce them to their primal elements. In the towns and cities the people put on their winter coats and hunched their shoulders against the cold wet pressure of an early winter. In the Canfield house the burning logs in the fireplace spread their warmth and comfort in defiance against the outside world. The talk now was about Christmas. Some of the boarders were going home to spend the holidays with their families. The printer arranged special discounts for those who wanted greeting cards that would bear their formally engraved names. One of the lodgers initiated a modest pool to buy a household present for Ma and Pa, and another talked about putting some colorful decorations in the windows. For Mr. Hemphill things were looking up. He got a job for the Saturdays before the pre-Christmas rush at a department store selling shoes, and as business increased during the week before Christmas he worked every day.

One night, at Ma's urging, he placed a telephone call to his family in the East. To hear their voices and expressions of love made him feel good, and yet there was shame, too, in having to confess that he could not send them anything for Christmas. No, he couldn't come home yet for awhile. Yes, his health was good, though he did now and then feel that old pain in his chest when the tensions and worries were most pressing. Yes, he would take care of himself and come home as soon as he could.

On the night before Christmas his temporary job ended, and once again he stood alone against the world. It was as if a long tentacle of the great financial crash had reached out to catch him once again. Like a man dying of thirst he had had one drink of water that had only for a moment revived his hope for life, but the vast desert still lay ahead. He had earned twenty-five dollars at the store. Part of it he gave to the Canfields as a token payment for his keep, and the rest he stored carefully away to be used for going home. It was a start, but despite the high spirits and revelry around him on Christmas Day he felt depressed. His thoughts alternated between despair and courage. The spirit had surrendered, but the mind kept saying this was no time to give up. Something was bound to happen, perhaps just around the corner.

A new year came and the Canfield household returned to normal. Mr. Hemphill continued to look for work. Despite the mid-winter slump, Ma Canfield drove him out to follow any lead that anyone might suggest. She knew for a certainty that with all his rich experience someone would recognize the skills he had to offer. And so it came to pass that one day her prediction came true. On an almost deserted back street he found a place where his plight seemed to be understood. It was a small establishment that sold hardware and household gadgets. Some of the items were manufactured in a shop, at the rear, where the owner worked on his inventions when he was not tending the store. No, he didn't really need any help, but he understood what it was like to be out of work and broke. But if Mr. Hemphill wanted to try his hand at selling door-to-door, there might be something they could work out.

The item to be sold was a metal door latch that the inventor had "perfected" in his shop, but of which he now had an over supply. The item did not sell, and the proprietor wanted to get rid of his stock. The gadget in question was very much like the kind of latch commonly found in apartment houses—a small brass plate to be screwed fast to the door jamb, with a short chain that could be secured to a slot in another brass plate fastened to the door. The only unique features of this device were that the chain was encased in a cloth sheath and the brass plates were carved in a decorative shape. "People will love 'em if they see 'em," the shopkeeper said. "They should sell for two dollars apiece retail. I'll let you have all you want for a dollar each, and you can double your money." Hemphill had five dollars to invest in the enterprise.

That night there was great rejoicing at the Canfield house. The five precious objects were examined and admired. Ma Canfield declared that Mr. Hemphill was a super-salesman and his beautiful door fasteners would sell like hotcakes. One of the students brought out an old briefcase in which the new salesman could carry his stock-in-trade, and Ma decreed that he should start first thing in the morning. The dying embers of hope flickered and flamed up again.

The next day Hemphill started out on his new enterprise. A cold wind blew in from the north bringing rain and sleet that cut through the thin overcoat he wore. He boarded a streetcar downtown, and the temporary shelter gave him some relief from the outside chill. He was headed for the end of the line where the streetcar stopped to let off its last passengers and reverse its trolley to head back into the city. This was a residential area in a separate municipality outside the city limits, a likely place for the novice salesman to try his luck.

The houses suggested a respectable middle-class neighborhood with an air of neatness that was marred here and there by boxes of gay wrapping paper and discarded Christmas trees piled near the curb for the trash wagon to haul away. Hemphill rehearsed his sales pitch and began to ring doorbells. Good morning, Ma'am. I wonder if you would be interested in something I have for you today that will bring you a little more peace of mind at night or when you are away from home. This is a lovely home you have here, and I know you want to protect yourself from burglars or unwanted visitors. In these troubled times we all need security. Security, that's what we need.

After two hours he had sold one door latch. By mid-afternoon he had sold a second and had made a profit of two dollars. His shoes were wet and his feet were cold, and the chill of the wind cut into him; it was time to give up for the day and go home. Back at the Canfield house that night Ma declared that he had made a good start and things would go better tomorrow. When Pa came home at midnight he remarked, privately of course, that if Hemphill could "cut the mustard" and had the "stick-to-it-iveness" to build up a little nest-egg, maybe he could work his way out of the corner he was in.

The next day was the same as the first. The rain had slackened but the wind was just as cold, and from time to time Hemphill felt a wave of dizziness sweep into his brain and he would have to rest until it passed. He went back to the same residential area to continue offering a commodity that no one seemed to want; but he persisted, and by mid-day he had sold his three remaining door latches. He felt some pride in the accomplishment; he had earned five dollars in the two days. Tomorrow he would replenish his stock and try again.

As he waited for the streetcar to take him back to the security of the Canfield house, he was approached by a man who seemed to have been following him for some time, a short, bulky, round-faced man wearing heavy galoshes and a long overcoat that was a little too tight. Hemphill's first thought was that the stranger was about to ask for money. Too bad if he did; the fellow would certainly be out of luck this time.

"You're new around this neighborhood," the man said. The statement was direct and without preliminaries, and Hemphill thought he caught a note of threatening belligerence in the voice.

"Yes, I am."

"Yes, I've had my eye on you. What are you selling?"

Hemphill briefly explained as much as he considered necessary, and then added with an impulse of naive pride that he had taken in ten dollars, with a five-dollar profit for his two days of work.

"So you are a salesman," the man said. "Well, I am an officer of the law, and in this town you need a peddler's license to sell stuff door-to-door. Do you have a license?"

"No, I didn't know that." A new sense of danger swept into his mind, and he began to feel the throbbing of his heart in his temples.

"Well, ignorance of the law is no excuse. And being an officer, I've got to enforce the town's ordinances," the fat man said. He flipped open a wallet revealing a badge.

"How much does the license cost?" Hemphill felt the world beginning to close in on him again.

"Twenty dollars for the license," the man said, "but I'll have to take you in to face the municipal judge, and he'll fine you ten dollars for what you have been doing."

"I don't have twenty dollars. Is there no other way out of this situation?" Hemphill's heart was beating faster now, and a sharp pain stabbed his chest. Should he argue? Should he plead? Should he submit?

"Well, I can't sell you the license, but I guess I could save you from goin' down to see the judge. You could give me the ten-dollar fine, and I could turn it in for you. That would spare you a lot of trouble. I don't see no better way to get you out of the spot you're in."

Arthur Hemphill was tired.

Riding back to the city Hemphill was not consciously aware of the clattering of the streetcar or the shelter it gave him from the chilling rain that had once again begun to drive with slanting force against the forlorn houses that seemed to huddle against it along the lifeless street. He was seeing, instead, something he had somehow witnessed before, or been a part of, the scene of a lonely man sitting on a stone bench in front of a far-off public library, thinking of a long black tunnel that had no end.

At the boarding house that night the gentle words of sympathy drifted through his consciousness like waves that came and went in vague whorls. The pain in his chest tightened around his heart, and he collapsed. He sensed the tender care with which he was put to bed, and then the hushed voices around him floated off and became those of his wife and children from somewhere far away.

The doctor came, but there was little that could be done. "A severe cardiac problem and a massive stroke," the doctor said. A sheet was spread gently over his face, and Arthur Hemphill went home. But not to Boston.

The Legend of
Chief Little Sitting Bear

"OH, RANGER, how many undiscovered Indian ruins are there out in the desert there?" Well, the last time we counted them there were just five hundred and sixty-seven undiscovered ones, not to mention the lost ruins we already know about. "Oh, Ranger, if I drive up this road to the end of it in this canyon, are you sure we can turn around up there?" Well, If you couldn't we'd have a lot of people up there, wouldn't we? "Oh, Ranger, how do porcupines make love?" Very carefully.

Visitors to our national parks are always asking questions, most of which are sensible and penetrating, calling for the best knowledge the ranger can offer. But now and then someone will come up with a query that is either very naive or outright stupid, and if the ranger has a sense of humor the answer can be a bit waggish. And occasionally an honest and valid question will evoke a good story, and the ranger will tell the tourists what he thinks they want to hear rather than the honorable truth. There is a maxim in life, which every politician knows all too well, that if you tell people what they want to hear, they will believe it. How this precious gem of wisdom was revealed to me can be told in a story of epic proportions about such a creative deception. If you will come with me a safe distance back in time to one of our great national parks, I'll tell you how it all happened.

I don't know what the bureaucratic hierarchy is now, but when I had a rather tenuous connection with the U.S. National Park Service many years ago there were in the western parks three kinds of rangers. First were the forest rangers who worked for the Department of Agriculture protecting the ecology of the region. They wore the same green uniforms as the park rangers, and in the public mind "forest ranger" was the generic term for all rangers.

There were also the park rangers, who tended to the management of the parks, which were operated by the Department of the Interior. They collected the fees at the park entrances, maintained law and order, and kept people from eating the wild animals and vice versa. The third, and in our snobbish view the most elite echelon of this eclectic caste system, were the ranger-naturalists. Highly trained in the sciences that gave each park its unique character—geology, anthropology, archaeology, botany, zoology, history, and the like—they handled the educational programs of the area, did research, lectured at museums, led caravans and walking parties of sightseers (privately referred to as "dudes") along the trails, and answered all questions that park visitors might ask whether they were sensible or not. I was a ranger-naturalist. Not a genuine full-time naturalist, but one of those "ninety-day-wonders" who came in during the summer months when the tourist season was heaviest. For me and others like me, it was pleasant outdoor work during the gap between academic years at the university. The schedule coincided perfectly with the school year, the pay was pretty good, the environment was pleasant, the park visitors were at their leisurely best—for the time being, not having to act like bankers or lawyers or salesmen or stenographers or schoolteachers—and the handsome uniforms we wore were attractive to the ladies.

Although I had served in two other places, I think my favorite was Glacier National Park. I usually managed to get my assignment as far away from Park Headquarters as possible; this gave me freedom from the critical eye of my boss, the Chief Park Naturalist. So it came to pass that I was stationed at Many Glacier Lodge, which is in the far northeast corner of the Park, while the headquarters were at Belton forty miles away at the southwest corner.

There were three of us at Many Glacier—Reinecke, Blondeau, and I—but Reinecke didn't count; he had his family with him that summer and they lived in a cabin in the campground. Blondeau and I shared a cabin, planned the programs, and were "in charge," if that flattering term ever needed to be used. The three of us took turns lecturing in the evenings at the Lodge and guiding trail trips mornings and afternoons. As part of our routine, therefore, every morning at nine o'clock we would meet our trail party in front of the Lodge and give them a short introductory lecture about the history of the Park.

Next we would lead them on a "Nature Walk" southward along a trail that passed through a forested area where we could give them the usual spiel: "That's a tree ... That's a flower ... That's a bird." Of course, we were a little more specific than that, sometimes with great virtuosity demonstrating our impressive knowledge of the species, variety, and ecological significance of each phenomenon of nature. Our trail then swung westward, over an impressive glacial moraine where we could explain the effects of glaciation. Here, too, we could identify by name and Indian legend the various mountain peaks left standing on the landscape after the glaciation had had its way.

Further on, the trail followed a little stream fed from the glacier above, milky white with *Gletschermilch* or pulverized rock made fine as flour by the grinding of the heavy glacial ice. Here we were geologists talking about cirques, cols, aretes, and other words found only in crossword puzzles but all clearly demonstrable from that point. Our educational adventure ended at the edge of a little lake where we could look up to the great Grinnell Glacier lying at the foot of the Continental Divide, or as we called it the Garden Wall, rising two thousand perpendicular feet above us. Here we would be inspired by the grandeur of the scene, and after our little speech the people always applauded in joyful appreciation.

At this point something else invariably happened. On the skyline high above us a little thumb of rock stood out clearly against the blue sky. Always someone in the party would ask, "Oh, Ranger, what is the name of that formation up there?"

We had no answer, and the climax of the occasion was always blunted somewhat by their disappointment. Blondeau and I searched the *Manual,* which was our reference Bible on all matters pertaining to the natural history of the Park. Nothing. We looked through all the popular books sold in the gift shop at the Lodge but found nothing. Obviously the historians, the Park Service, and the Great Northern Railroad which fed the park most of its tourists had overlooked this important feature.

One night in our cabin Blondeau and I were talking about the problem, which we both had experienced. "The people want a story," I said.

"Yes, but there is nothing in the literature to give them one," Blondeau said. He was a plant physiologist by training and a scientist by nature; he always wanted to find the facts.

"Nevertheless," I said, "the people want a story. Maybe we should give them one."

"Maybe we should," he agreed, proving that a scientist can also have a sense of humor if the price is right. "It might be fun to give them an Indian legend."

We talked about it long into the night, and by morning we had the answer. Glacier National Park was about to give birth to a new legend. It happened to be my turn the next morning, and I was ready. I met my group at the lodge as usual. We walked around the forest edge and talked about the trees, birds, squirrels, and rocks. We crossed the moraine and talked about the place names. We walked along the stream and discussed the powers and effects of glaciation. At the little lake we looked up at Grinnell Glacier lying above that. I ended the lecture, and the people applauded as enthusiastically as ever. I waited.

Finally a lady said, "Ranger, is there any name for that formation up there?" She pointed to the thumb of rock, and everybody looked. "Yes, there is a story about that, an old legend the Blackfeet Indians used to tell. Would you like to hear it?"

"Oh, yes," they all said. They crowded in close to hear the story.

"Well, once upon a time," I began, "there was an Indian village in a big canyon on the other side of the Garden Wall from here. It was a happy village. The old chief was wise and the people had plenty of game for food. They lived in peace with their neighbors, and their children played in the forest. The old chief had a beautiful daughter, and it was natural that all the young braves of the village wanted to marry her.

"One day there came a visitor from another tribe that was located down near Lake McDonald just above where the town of Belton is now. He was a handsome young man with all the skills he needed to become a chief himself some day. He stayed longer than he had first intended because the old chief's daughter had all the skills she needed to become the woman of a chief. As might be expected, they fell in love and would meet secretly by a little stream near the village to talk and dream and make their plans.

"One day the young visitor went to the old chief and asked for his daughter in the custom of marriage, as the traditions of the people required. But to their surprise the old chief said no. There could be no marriage for these two because of the clan to which the boy belonged. It was taboo for anyone in the old chief's clan to marry anyone from that particular tribe. So the answer was no, and the lovers had to conceal their disappointment. But no matter what the obstacles are, young love will find a way." At this point I made the romantic elements as juicy as I could, dripping with sentimentality, and I spread the concoction as thick as possible. I was "on a roll," as they say in show business, and the audience loved it.

"They made their plans," I went on, "and one night at about midnight they stole out of the village together. They had packed only the most necessary things to take with them, and they chose the trail that led not southward to Lake McDonald, but this way straight toward the steep divide. They knew they had to hurry, for when the old chief discovered that they were gone he would surely follow, and his vengeance would be terrible. Too soon he knew what had happened, and he started up the trail after them. They climbed as fast as they could, but they knew the old chief was gaining on them. They reached the top and came over the divide just above Grinnell Glacier. You can see from here the little pass through which they came. "Without stopping to rest, they hurried down this way right across the glacier. About midway, they looked back and saw that the angry father had reached the top. It had been a hard climb, and he sat down on a rock to catch his breath. They should not have looked back for just at that moment the young lovers slipped and fell into a deep crevasse and were lost forever.

"The Great Spirit had been watching, and when the tragedy happened he was very angry. He pointed his finger at the old father and put a curse on him. He said, 'Chief Little Sitting Bear, you must stay sitting on that rock until the glacier yields up the bodies of these young lovers!' And there he sits to this day. That's Chief Little Sitting Bear."

The audience applauded more enthusiastically than they had done before, and we all went our way. Back at the Lodge, I reported in.

"Did you tell the story?" Blondeau asked.

"Yes."

"How did it go over?"

"Pretty well, I think."

So the next day, Blondeau told the same story. He got an equally favorable reaction. "Shall we tell Reinecke?" I asked.

"Not yet. Let's not clutter up his mind with such things just now. We ought to try it once more before we spread it." But that never happened.

On the morning of the third day, Blondeau had gone to the Lodge for breakfast and I was sleeping late. Suddenly there was a banging at the door. I jumped up, and there striding through the door was Walker, the Chief Naturalist, our boss. He had left Park

Headquarters early and had driven the forty miles from Belton over Logan Pass and up to Many Glacier that morning.

"What the hell is this I hear about some Chief Little Sitting Bear?" he demanded.

"What about it?" I asked. "Do you want a cup of coffee?"

"No, I don't want a cup of coffee. I want an explanation about some yarn you and Blondeau are spreading about a Chief Little Sitting Bear. People all over the Park are talking about it."

"What's the matter? It's a good story, isn't it?"

"Maybe so, but it's a fake. It's not in the literature."

"Well, the legend of Going-to-the-Sun Mountain is not a real Indian legend, either. It was put out by the Great Northern Railroad to attract tourists."

"That may be, but it's in the official literature. You can tell that one, but you've got to stop telling these lies about some imaginary Chief Little Sitting Bear."

The message was clear. The establishment had spoken, and we didn't tell the story anymore. But I always took comfort in the fact that two trail parties somewhere in America had heard the Blackfeet legend of the lost lovers.

But that's not the end of the story. Twenty years later, while giving a lecture, I told this tale. Afterwards a lady in the audience came up and said, "I've heard that story before."

"You have? Where?"

"My aunt told me that legend when I was just a little girl. She had been to Glacier National Park and had heard it there."

"When was she in Glacier?" I asked. The lady thought for a moment and then told me the year as nearly as she could remember. It was the same year that Blondeau and I had brought Little Sitting Bear into petrified immortality.

So the legend lived on. The folk had triumphed over the establishment after all.

On Becoming Somebody

I WANT TO TELL you this story because I think it will make you feel good, and because it's true. There are no tricks of the storyteller's craft in it, no hidden symbolism, no contrived crises leading to a climax, no subtle foreshadowing of things to come. This is just the way it happened.

One summer I was invited to teach a seminar in American Folklore at a university in Southern California. I was a little late in arriving on campus, and the students had already registered for their courses when I went to the office of the English Department to pick up my list of enrollees. Several of the regular faculty members were sitting around having coffee, and their greeting was cordial.

"Let's have a look at your roll sheet," one of them said. "We're curious to see who has signed up for your course." They knew their senior and graduate students and were eager to tell me what they could about them. I was getting the impression that I would have a very good class when suddenly the professors gave the list a double-take look.

"Oh, no," one of the sighed. "You've got Joe Murtha."

"What's a Joe Murtha?" I asked.

"He's the most belligerent, obnoxious student on campus," he said. "Joe dominates the class, argues with the teacher, intimidates the other students with his sarcasm, and whether he's right or wrong he insists on having his way. He's nothing but trouble. He manages to pass his courses and he'll probably graduate, but look out for him; he'll kill your class." The other professors nodded in sympathetic agreement.

When the class met, about ten students in the seminar, I was able to recognize Joe immediately. He sat at the far end of the table, opposite to me, and no other students sat near him. Obviously they knew of his reputation and wanted to dissociate themselves from him, and I sensed that he knew it. He listened to what was being said, but did not take notes or join in the discussion. From what I had been told, I expected some overt resistance to either me or the material, but there was no indication of that. The field of folklore was new to him, and I decided that he was waiting to be sure of his ground before he pounced.

As the course progressed through the first week and I was laying the foundation for the understanding of folklore with definitions, concepts, and references on the moot questions of scholarship, Joe spoke very little. He came to class regularly and asked questions occasionally, but his inquiries were usually to make sure that he understood procedural matters and requirements rather than to clarify substantive issues. Apparently he was not the ogre I had been warned about. At least, not yet.

One requirement in the course was that each student must collect some folklore from an informant or two who knew ballads, tales, superstitions, customs, or ethnic traditions that would add to our materials of folk culture. Most of the students found their informants and began the experience of collecting. But not Joe. One day I asked him to wait after class to talk about it. By way of finding some fertile ground for him I asked, "Joe, what is your ethnic background?"

As he stood before me I thought of the caricature that had been planted in my mind, a belligerent hulk with a low brow, fierce scowling face, and clenched fists. And yet there was something else about him that seemed to contradict this biased perception of his external appearance, and I wondered how much his professors had been influenced by an image that might be concealing a sensitive and vulnerable person.

"I don't know much about my ethnic background," he said. "My father was Indian, but he cut out when I was little." Joe was looking, not at me but through me, as if toward something far away. Then quickly his eyes came back to me. "I tell people I'm Italian because that seems to impress them, but my mother was really English if you go way back. The truth is, I guess I'm just an Okie. We came from the dust bowl country." He paused, waiting for my reaction, but I gave none. "I still live with my mother. She's just an Okie from the back country. She used to live somewhere in the Ozarks."

"Then why don't you collect some of the customs and beliefs of the mountain folk where your mother lived?"

"No, I don't think I'd care to mess with that stuff." He paused, and I waited for more. "You see, there is a kind of community of Okies here, all right, but they're just hillbillies. I'm trying to get away from that kind of life. They might have a lot of folklore, plenty of superstitions, but I never thought it was worth much. Let's just say I've rejected all that."

"And your friends, who are they?"

"I have friends, but they are not Okies or Mexicans or Indians. I never bring my friends home with me if I can help it. There's only my mother there, and she, well, she's just a backwoods person. She can't any more than write her own name."

"Do you talk with her much?"

"No, not much. I eat and sleep there, but that's about all." And that was all Joe seemed to want to say on the subject of his personal life. Besides collecting folklore from informants, another of the aims of my course was to help the students develop a sense of the worth of the ordinary person. In America, legendary heroes are usually common people who have found greatness—workers, soldiers, pioneers, or the oppressed—not gods or kings; moreover, it is often the common person who is the best carrier of his traditional culture. Such an individual can contribute to our knowledge and pleasure more than he may ever realize, and through such a contribution find the identity, recognition, and appreciation that the person may need. In this way, often a nobody can become a somebody with a gift that is appreciated.

To illustrate this point I told the class a story that I had heard Professor Thelma James of Wayne State University in Detroit relate at a conference several years earlier. It was about a young couple who had come from Poland to settle in Detroit and work in a factory there. They had good jobs and prospered in the American scene, learned the language, bought a home, and talked about raising a family. Because things were going so well for them they often said, "Wouldn't it be nice if Papa and Mama could come over here and live with us." Papa and Mama were just poor peasants in the Old Country. They had worked hard all their lives and now they deserved the ease and comfort of life in America.

It took time to arrange all the necessary papers, but at last Papa and Mama came to Detroit to live with their son and his wife. It was a happy reunion, and they enjoyed their release from toil and hardship. But as the months passed, things changed. The friends of their children were not their friends. They did not know the language, so Papa could not go to the store to buy things, and Mama did not dare even to answer the door bell. On social occasions when visitors came and there was a party, Papa and Mama could not join in. They were only stupid creatures from another world and an embarrassment to their children. Finally it was suggested that when company came Papa and Mama might be happier if they stayed out in the kitchen.

At last the time came when the two old people found themselves assigned to a little apartment upstairs at the back of the house, cared for but otherwise forgotten. They would sit long hours with nothing to do, and their thoughts turned back to their lives in the Old Country. The work had been hard in Poland, the winters were cold, food was scarce, and sickness was often fatal; and yet they had good friends there. In their loneliness they began to wish they had never left home.

Then a day came when Professor James and her class in folklore came to visit the Polish couple. They had heard that these people might be good informants from whom they could collect Polish lore in America. But the young couple had forgotten many of their native traditions. They knew some of the songs, but many of the verses they could not remember. They knew about the dances, but some of the figures and steps were a little uncertain.

"We learned these things from Papa and Mama. Maybe they can help you more than we can."

So as a special privilege, Papa and Mama were allowed to come down and meet the folklorists. Did Mama know that lovely old lullaby? Yes, she did, and she sang it through for them. She knew dozens of little songs, and she sang them all. Did Papa remember that game or dance? Yes, he did, and he demonstrated every turn of the game and step of the dance. It was discovered that Papa and Mama were a treasure trove of Polish folklore, and they became the center of attention. Their contribution was so valuable that scholars heard about them as far away as the University of Chicago. They even got their picture in the newspaper. And from that day on, Papa and Mama were no longer mere nobodies; they had become persons once again.

When I finished the story, the class was over and the students drifted out. Only Joe remained behind. I noticed that his eyes were glistening, and he self-consciously brushed his cheek with the back of his finger.

"Yes, Joe?" I asked.

"That story," he began, and then hesitated a long thoughtful moment. "Well, you know," he continued cautiously. "I have always denied my background. I would never even invite my friends home because I was, well, I guess ashamed of my mother. She's just a simple woman. But when I was little she used to sing me some songs that I liked. I don't remember what they are about, but they might be good. Do you think it would be all right if I interviewed my mother and maybe taped some of her songs?" Joe was cautiously feeling his way.

"By all means, Joe," I said. "Get acquainted with your mother and collect those songs from her."

A few days passed. When Joe reported on his progress he was guardedly enthusiastic. "I'm taping my mother's songs now," he said. "I didn't know she knew so many. They are pretty good, too."

"Then you and your mother are spending a lot of time together now," I ventured.

"Oh, yes. She is very glad that I am recording them."

"What kind of songs are they?"

"Well, they seem mostly to be old English and Scottish ballads. Some of them are the same as those collected by Professor Child and published in his book of English and Scottish popular ballads found in America. Some of them don't seem to be in print anywhere, but they must go back to the middle ages. I'll have to check into that."

A few more days went by. He and his mother were working long hours together now, getting her songs on the tape and checking them against all such ballads he could find in print. He also found that very little research had been done on the tunes, which were, after all, a most essential part of folk songs.

"Do you sing, Joe? Have you learned any of them for yourself?"

"I guess I can, a little. I've never really tried. But some of those ballads are beautiful, and I've learned one or two."

Joe's research was beginning to fascinate him. It took him into musicology, a field new to him. And he studied the variants among all the published collections and began to compare them in terms of the story told, the characters involved, and the local versions that suggested factors in the process of transplantation from England and Scotland to America. When he made his report to the class his findings were astonishing. He had delved into the musical phrasing, the artistic pattern of certain refrains, the "leaping and lingering" movement of the story, the musical transitions between speakers in the ballad, and the relation of musical modes and cadences to the song. These old ballads had endured for centuries and had traveled from country to country, and had finally reached California through the memory and voice of his mother. His own mother! Joe had found a priceless treasure, and it had lit up his mind with a fire that he had never felt before. He even sang one or two of the songs, himself, to illustrate his points.

After his report to the class, several of the students congratulated him. He didn't know quite how to respond to such expressions of approval; he merely shrugged his shoulders and grunted. But for the first time, I saw Joe smile.

When the term ended, the university held graduation exercises for the Summer Session students. I caught Joe in the hall one day and to make conversation I said, "I see that your name is on the list of graduates, Joe. Will I see you in the academic parade?"

"Oh, no. I've never intended to go. It's just a ritual that's a lot of nonsense, and I don't go in for that kind of thing."

"What does your mother think about it?"

"Oh, she's pleased, of course. But even if she went to the graduation she wouldn't understand what was going on."

"You might be surprised, Joe," I ventured.

"Well, maybe." Again he was feeling his way through a new situation on dangerous ground.

On the final day the traditional ceremony was enacted. I marched with the faculty in the splendor of our full regalia, and when the graduates filed onto the platform to receive their degrees, there was Joe in his cap and gown with the rest of them. He had shed his role of detachment and was playing a new and happier part.

After the recessional, as usual the joyful graduates were floating around in their black robes greeting friends, hugging relatives, and gathering in little clusters for pictures. And there, too, was Joe. He saw me and came over for the customary congratulatory handshake.

"I wasn't going to come," he apologized," but my mother wanted to see me graduate. I wonder if it would be all right if I introduced her to you?"

"Of course, Joe. I'd love to meet your mother."

He disappeared around the corner of a building and returned ushering his mother to where I was standing. She was a little woman, obviously prematurely old from years of hard work. Her dress was plain and somewhat old-fashioned, but she had the spotlessly clean starched and ironed look that told me this was her very best and she had taken great pains to appear like a queen. Our conversation was short, but as we shook hands I could see that no mother was ever more proud.

We said good-bye and went our different ways. I never saw Joe again. But I heard from other sources that he had gone on to a major university and earned his Ph.D., using his mother's songs and deeper research on popular ballads in America as his doctoral dissertation. Later I learned that he had gained some reputation as a folk singer. And finally I heard that he was teaching in a college and writing a book.

Joe had found himself. But what was more important, he had discovered that his mother was somebody after all.

The Slaves of Stony Creek

HE COULD STILL see her, that little old Indian woman sitting on her blanket in the shade of a big oak tree that stood beside her withering shack. Her wrinkled, palsied hands resting against her apron were gnarled and brown like the dead leaves on the ground beside her, and the bony fingers curled as if they could not unclasp the phantom handle of some long-forgotten tool. It seemed to him, as he looked at her with a child's eyes, that she must have been a hundred years old. Her hair was white and thin, her face was dark and dry like brown paper that had been crumpled, and the wrinkles etching her mouth and chin and forehead were deep in the loose skin. Her old eyes seemed small and almost hidden in sunken sockets that made her peer searchingly into the subtle shadows as if he were about to disappear. And yet despite that furtive squint those aged eyes shone with a brightness that almost twinkled with the mysterious beauty of the first stars in the twilight afterglow of sunset. Old though she was, she seemed somehow alive and vibrant and beautiful. Perhaps the fact that she was his grandmother made the difference.

He was part Indian and as a child he had an Indian name, but that doesn't matter. People just called him Sharkey. His grandmother once had an Indian name, too, but when he knew her she had become Maria. That's what the Spaniards called her when she was their slave, and that was good enough to take her through life. So this is Maria's story, not Sharkey's, as she told it to him with an ancient sadness in her heart that day from her store-bought blanket under the oak tree.

She was a child born of the dawning in the village of the Che-e-voka, or Salt People, where the wickiups squatted in a shallow canyon beside a deep stream that the white people, when they came, called Stony Creek. It flowed eastward across the wide valley to the big river that swept down from the north, which the white people called the Sacramento. The Che-e-voka lived well, hunting deer and rabbits for meat and hides, catching fish from the deep waters of the creek, snaring wild birds that flew down from the north or that lived in the low bushes of the hillside, and digging sweet roots to flavor the acorns the women ground at the grinding stone. They were called salt people because near the creek was a ledge of rock that held salt, and other tribes came to trade for it. The Wintoon from the high mountain of always snow, where the great river started, would stop on their way to trade with the Miwoc at a place the Spaniards called Bodega, and they brought the shiny black stone for making spearheads and arrow points, and on their way back they would bring sea shell beads, which were like money. When she was a child Maria had learned to play the games and sing the songs of her people. And the night birds sang for her, and the flowering shrubs gave forth the deep-breathing joy of sweet odors, and the children laughed and squealed at their games. When she was a young girl her mother taught her how to make baskets like those of the Pomo and to grind acorns for food, and soften the animal skins for making winter robes. And when she became a woman she learned to walk tall like a woman, and she was slim and graceful. And the young man who made her feel like a woman, whose name was Red Bush, was a fast runner and strong and handsome. And according to the ways of their grandfathers they were married, and his spirit came into her and she trembled. And life was good.

Then came the day when the Spaniards rode into the village. The people tried to run and hide, but the Spaniards lassoed them from their horses and dragged them to one place, and when some people fought back the Spaniards killed them. They shot them with their guns. But to the old ones they would say, "Go away. We don't want you." And to the little children they said, "Go away. We don't want you." But the young people were tied with ropes braided from horsehair, and they had to stand there and wait till the Spaniards were satisfied that they had the ones they wanted. And Maria stood with them.

But her young man Red Bush was not there. He had gone hunting and was somewhere in the hills when the Spaniards came. Maria looked for him but he was not there, and she was glad because she loved him. For herself, though, she was afraid. No one could tell what was going to happen or how soon, maybe, they would be killed. Then the Spaniards tied them together with the long ropes knotted around their necks with spaces between so they could walk in a line. When they got outside the village they saw some other Spaniards waiting for them, and they had also on long ropes several of the young Bloody Rock people, who were their neighbors over the hill. So they were all taken and led southward.

They had to walk on unknown trails. The village of the salt people, where they had felt the warm fires of home, disappeared behind the hills. The trees that had given them shade and the big rocks that had hidden the secret places where they had played were lost behind them, and the unseen spirits of strange places clouded their minds.

All day they walked, and their feet were sore from the sharp stones, and their necks hurt from the ropes. But if they tried to stop, the Spaniards whipped them. One Spaniard was the big man who had the power, and his men called him Berryessa, and sometimes he would tell his men to let the Indians stop and rest, and sometimes he told them to give the Indians a drink of water. All day they walked. Over the hills and among the rocks they walked, going always to the south. Maria and her people were tired and hungry, and they could have no private time and they were ashamed. But the guards with their guns were always there.

The hot sun sank away and it was evening, and the Spaniards made camp for the night. They built campfires and cooked the meat of a deer they had killed that day, and they let the Indians eat. Before it was too dark to see, some of Maria's friends whispered, "Look," and with their eyes they showed her where to look, and among some big rocks nearby she saw him. It was Red Bush, her man, hiding behind the rocks. Then she knew that he had come back from his hunting and found them gone. He had followed them, always keeping out of sight of the Spaniards. What could be his plan? She didn't know. She hoped he would not let the Spaniards see him, or they would shoot him.

That night the Spaniards made them lie in circles around three campfires with their legs tied together at the ankles. The women they did not tie up, and they could sleep near their men who were tied together. They could whisper to each other, but no one could say where they were going. Two of the Bloody Rock people, a young man and his woman, made signs that they were going to run away, but Maria was afraid for them. They whispered that they would rather die than live as captive slaves on a rope. So when it was near daylight before the sun came up they crept away. The woman had a hidden knife, and she cut the rope that held her man, and they crawled off into the brush. But the Spaniards saw them go and ran after them, and they shot them. When they were dead and they lay there side by side, the Spaniards shouted, "See what will happen to you if you try to escape."

After the morning food the Spaniards started to tie the women together as they had been the day before, but Berryessa said, "No, that is not necessary now." So the women that had been tied up were united so that they could walk beside their men. And when a Spaniard came to untie Maria he stood behind her and pulled her head back by the hair with one hand, and with the other hand he reached over her shoulder and held her breast, and he pulled her head back so her face was next to him. And Maria knew that Red

Bush was watching from his hiding place, and she was ashamed. Then Berryessa saw what the man was trying to do, and he said, "No. Not here. Not now." So the man left her alone. Then they began their long walk again, always southward.

When they stopped at mid-day to rest and take food and water from a little stream, Maria looked at the trees and rocks on the hillside, and when she saw something move up there she looked again and she saw Red Bush. He was hiding behind some trees, and when he saw her looking he made a sign to her. But she could not tell what he was trying to say.

All day they walked, and their feet were tired. At sunset they made camp and built fires to cook the food. That day the Spaniards had killed a bear, so they cooked the bear for food that night. But the Salt People said, "We cannot eat this meat because it is taboo. Our great-grandfather was of the bear kind, and we do not eat the flesh of our own people." But they were hungry and there was nothing else, so they ate the roasted flesh of the bear and it made them sick. Maria knew that somewhere out in the brush of the hillside Red Bush would be watching, and she wondered whether he would have eaten the forbidden meat.

The next morning as the Spaniards were getting them ready for the day's long walk, a new thing happened. Everybody looked up at the hillside, and there was Red Bush. He was coming toward the camp. He had one hand high in the air, and in the other hand he held his bow and arrow out in front of him. So the Spaniards let him come, and he was made a captive, too. And when he came by Maria's side he touched her hand, and she knew that he loved her more than his life. She was glad, but also she was sad for him.

More days they walked, and at last they came to a place where there were many houses of the white people, and one was a big house bigger than Maria had ever imagined a house could be. And around it were walking many men wearing long brown robes with white ropes tied around the middle, and they did not wear boots like the Spaniards but flat sandals on their feet. There was much talk between the brown-robes and the Spaniards, and finally someone said to the Salt People, "You will stay here now. This is your home now. You will do what the brown-robes tell you to do, and you will work on the farms and in the houses of the white people. They are not Spaniards as you have thought, but Mexicans, and you will learn their language. The brown-robes you will call *fathers* and they will save your souls and teach you about God." And they said, "You should be very happy now. You will be like Mexicans. Your names will be Mexican. From now on your name will be called Maria." Then to Red Bush they said, "Your name will be Antonio, and you cannot be of the Che-e-voka any more forever." And to the others they said, "Your name will be Julian, and yours will be Guadalupe, and Angela, and Manuel, and Thomas, and Bonito, and Diego, and Malpero," and they told others like that. So they were not Che-e-voka or Bloody Rock people any more except in their secret hearts.

The men worked hard all day on the ranches of the Mexicans, and the women worked in the houses and sometimes also in the fields. If they did not work hard enough, men with whips would beat them. If some people tried to run away, men on horses would find them and bring them back and whip them in a place where everybody could see it. The fathers told the slave people all about God, and how their souls were being saved from something bad so they could be happy at some after-death time, but they never understood what it meant. They learned how to do the ceremonial things to please the brown-robe fathers, but they could never see the face nor hear the voice of the Mexican God as they had heard the voice of the wind in the trees speaking to them at home, or felt the spirits of the wild animals of the mountains. These new ceremonies were not like the songs and dances that had been handed down to them—the song welcoming the dawn and the song for the night when you end the day and the dawn brings the new life of the new day. In those times each song had a meaning, and the things they had learned in childhood were always with them. Their spirits were strengthened by these thoughts, and sometimes when they were alone they could clear their minds of all the new things and find strength in remembering the old ways.

Some years passed and Maria learned how to speak the Mexican language. Also she learned how to cook the Mexican food and make the Mexican clothing. She and Antonio were allowed to live together like married people, and so could the others who were married. The fathers were good about that. And sometimes the Indians could meet together and talk in their own language about the old ways. That's how it happened that they learned a very important thing. Thomas and Manuel had gone out with some Mexicans to find lost cattle, and when they came back they said that the mission village where they lived was near a big lake or ocean of water. They all talked about it, and someone thought that maybe the water came from the great river that was in the big valley near their home. Then someone said that if they could steal away and find that river they could follow it upstream and some day come to their own Stony Creek. This was worth thinking about, but it must be a magic secret.

Many times, when the hard work of the day was finished, they would sit in secret places and talk, and their thoughts always turned to their old homes in the hills. And Antonio said, "I think we can find our way back to the place of our fathers and mothers, to the place where we were free to be happy, and then we can breathe the air of our hills once more."

But Diego was afraid. He said, "It is not so bad here. We are given the food we eat and the clothes we wear. It is true we work hard, and sometimes we think of home with longing in our hearts, but we can never go back. The sun moves always the same way and does not go back. The seasons of the year move through life and death. The flowers have great beauty, but as the days of their lives pass they change and can never be the same again. It is so with us. We have been forced to change, and we can never be the same again. If we try to change it, we will be punished. It we try to run away, the Mexican soldiers will follow us and kill us. It would be better to live under the spell of the white man's God and work for these people until we are old, than to die now when we are young. I have said it."

Then Antonio spoke, and Maria sat by his side. He said, "It is not good for us to be here. We are like the wild bear that has been caught in a trap. We are like oxen that are forced to pull the plow with their heads down, and the spirit dies in us. We are like the horse that must carry the Mexican on his back and bleed from the spur. We are not the Che-e-voka any more, and we can never be Mexican. The God of the brown-robed fathers is not the spirit of our fathers, and the songs of these fathers are not the songs of our people." And the slave people nodded, for they felt the same way.

Then Antonio said more. "If the big river comes into this wide water, I think we can find it. If we are silent when we move, the Mexicans will not hear us. If we can hide, as the rabbit hides in the brush from the dogs, the soldiers will not find us. If we can move in the night and lie still in the day, the soldiers will look for us in other places. Then we can go home and be ourselves once more instead of oxen. But if we should die as we run away, I say we will then die as Che-e-voka and not as tame animals, I have said it."

Most of the slave people nodded yes, but some were afraid like Diego and said they would rather stay. Some said, "We have babies here, and to run or hide would be hard for them. So we will stay. Then Maria thought, "I am growing big with baby, but maybe there will be time if we go soon." Angela was thinking also the same thing, but they did not speak of it to the men, for it was bad to talk of such things. So they said, "We will go, but we must go before too long time." And those who said they would not go promised that they would not tell, and Antonio believed them.

So for the next many days and nights they hid food away for carrying, and some knives they put in hidden places. And after those many days and nights of whispering and thinking about it they were ready to steal away, and Maria was ready to go with Antonio, and some other women were ready to go with their men. And the friends of Diego who were afraid kept silent about it and did not tell.

On a night when there was no moon the Che-e-voka and a few of the Bloody Rock people crept under the shadows away from the mission and the Mexican guards. Like the grey fox that hunts at night they crouched under the darkness of the bushes and went quietly down to the place of the big water where Thomas and Manuel showed them to go. At first light they hid among the willows near the water, for they knew the soldiers would come to find them. And like the leader quail will sit on a high limb to guard over the other quail when they are on the ground to warn them if the owl is near or the wildcat is creeping to catch them, so Thomas found a high place to watch for the soldiers that would come to find them. And Angela his woman was with him.

When the Mexicans came on their horses looking for them, Thomas saw them coming and ran to warn his people, and all the Indians hid among the willows and covered up with sticks and leaves. They could hear the shouting of the soldiers and the sounds of horses coming through the brush, and they crouched down and were very still. Then after awhile the soldiers went on past and rode away, still looking for their slaves. But the Salt People did not make any noise, so the Mexicans did not find them. Then they felt like they were not slaves any more.

When it was safe they came out, and with their knives they cut willows and tules and made three canoes. And when it was night again they put their boats into the big water. Some of them rode in the canoes, some paddled, and some swam and clung to the boats. That way they crossed the big water. And when they found the river that flowed into it, they were not afraid any more, but still they moved at night and hid in the tules when it was daytime. For many days they followed up the river, and other rivers came into it, but they always chose the one that they thought came from the north. So after many days the river led them to a place that they had seen before. Far away they could see the mountain of everlasting snow, and then they knew they were coming to their home country.

When they found their own Stony Creek and the big rocks that they knew, their hearts were glad. But they were still careful because there could be other Mexicans coming along. When they came to the cliff of salty rock they knew they were home. When they saw the wickiups of their village they were too glad and made shouts to each other. But Antonio said "No, do not make a noise yet. The Mexicans could be here waiting to catch us again. Our people do not know we are coming, and they might think we are the enemy. Or maybe they are all dead. We must be careful here." So they were all quiet. And Antonio said, "You stay here, and I will first go alone and see what has happened here and tell them we are coming." And so he did that. After awhile he came back, and he put his hand to his mouth as a sign for them to be still. He said, "I have seen a bad thing that I do not understand. There are no people in our village. There were no old women or children in the wickiups. There were no old men in the ceremonial pit house. There were no dogs sleeping in the shade. What has become of our people I do not know."

Then Thomas spoke and said, "I think our people are still alive. I think we can find them. I think they have all gone up into the high mountains to the place where we had a hunting camp in the summer, and I think we should look for them there." So the tired travelers went up on an old trail into the high mountains. And after a long time they heard a shout, and they stopped to see what it was. Then came an old man running toward them. He was one of their people, and they were glad to see him. He told them he was a guard sent down the trail to watch for the Mexicans if they should come, and he told them that the Che-e-voka people and the Bloody Rock people had gone away from their old places and had made a new village hidden in the high mountains where the Mexicans could not find them.

So the slave people followed him to the new village, and when they saw their people again there was love in their hearts, and everybody was happy. And they told their story, and everybody said, "We will remember this a long time, and our children's children will hear about it. And after awhile Maria was the old one who told the story best, and she remembered it.

Maria brought out her baby, that was a girl child, and Angela also brought out her baby, and after the proper time they had other children, and so did the other women, and they were all Che-e-voka. But those who had been slaves remembered the language they had learned from the Mexicans, and they all kept the names that had been given to them, so Maria was always Maria after that, and Antonio was always Antonio. And Maria liked the food she had learned to cook, so for all the years after that she would make tortillas and other such food. And after some time other white men came who spoke another language that was not Mexican, and they also called the Indians by different names. So Maria and Antonio and the others had their first Indian names, their Mexican names, and the new names of the white people who settled in the valley. But that was all right. That way every Indian could be three people, and they felt no shame in it.

But the God of the Mexican fathers, that was also the God of the new white men,the Che-e-voka could never understand. They kept the old songs and the ceremonies of their fathers, and they felt good with the spirits of the trees and the animals around them and the sky and the clouds and the sun and the moon over them. They had no need for the ceremonial things that the Mexican fathers had made them do.

And whenever Maria would tell her story she would always say, "Remember that if you are Che-e-voka you will always be Che-e-voka, and people cannot make you what you are not, and you can be proud of that. And if you are caught in a trap when you can't help it, and you have to suffer in the body and in the spirit, remember that the suffering can make you strong. And if your mind is free to think the things that are natural for you, you will always be free inside no matter what other people make you do or say. And when you see around you what is good and what is bad, remember that what is good will stay in your heart and what is bad will go away. I have said it. "

There Could Be A Lesson
In It Somewhere

ACE MORGAN was a retired senior citizen. Retired from what wasn't too clear; his stories varied from time to time depending on the circumstances, usually determined by what his audiences wanted to hear. His Social Security check came regularly, and he spent much of his time down at the Senior Center swapping yarns with a few of the more talkative superannuates that haunted the place.

"The trouble is," he once said, "they're all tryin' to impress somebody with big brags about how important they used to be, or how hard they could fight, or how much money they made. They tell the same things over and over again, and they never want to listen to something really interesting, like when I fought with that bear up in Idaho or how I took Harold Ickes, the Secretary of the Interior, on a camping trip in Montana. No, those old birds that hang around the Senior Center are not very interesting. Just antiques. But some of the old ladies, though—well, that may be different."

Nevertheless, Ace Morgan went to the Center regularly. On Mondays he liked to play pool with a few special cronies; on

Wednesdays and Fridays he played bingo; on Thursdays he enjoyed just sitting on a bench under a tree, smoking his pipe and watching the gardener tend the flowers. It was on such a Thursday that Mrs. Forbes, the office manager, came looking for him.

"Oh, there you are, Mr. Morgan," she said. "I thought you might be around here somewhere. Somebody to see you." Three young people were following her into the garden. With a sweep of her hand, which was intended to serve as an introduction, she turned and left them.

They were teenagers—two girls and a boy. The girl in front had on a pair of faded blue jeans, her hair was a thick brown burr, and her countenance reminded him of the facial expression of a bird, a hawk wearing horn-rimmed glasses. The second girl had long yellow hair, a round doll-like face, and a figure which, while not exactly over-developed, was ripening fast. The boy was thin and angular with long legs—so long that Ace had to look twice to make sure he was not up on stilts. He's not an athlete, Ace thought; more the Gary Cooper type.

"I'm Margaret," said the horn-rimmed glasses.

"I'm Cindy," the China doll smiled with just the right touch of coyness.

"And this is Ted," the horn-rimmed glasses explained, and the stilts grinned in acknowledgement. "We're from Sequoia High School," Margaret went on, "and our English teacher, Mr. Murcheson, told us to come over here and maybe we could interview you."

"On what?" Ace liked to talk, but he was suspicious of such a formal situation as an interview in which he might be tricked into saying something that could be taken wrong.

"Well, we're supposed to be writing a feature story for our journalism class, and we were told that you could talk about what life was like in the Old West a long time ago."

"Why me?" Ace felt that there was a compliment in this somewhere, but he wanted to size up these young people before revealing too much of his personal life to them.

"We've heard that you tell some good stories about famous

western characters you have known," said the stilts. So the boy could talk, after all, Ace thought.

"Oh, I guess I could tell you a few things, all right. I used to know Death Valley Scotty and a few like that." It didn't take much to get Ace started if he had a willing audience, and apparently these young people were interested. "I've done a lot of things in my life that you high schoolers might get a kick out of. I've been bucked off my share of wild broncos, I've et wild rattlesnake out in Nevada, I've worked on the railroad up in Oregon, and I've done a little prospecting along the Colorado River. I've rounded up cattle in Utah, and I've pitched hay in Nevada. I've done just about everything except be a sailor; I never got to go to sea. And I've never herded sheep. I ain't got nothin' against sheepherders, you understand; I've known some mighty fine people that was sheep- herders, but I never got that desperate, myself."

"No, that's not quite what we want," said doll-face sweetly. "We're supposed to find out what life was like when, you know, you were like just a kid. What did you do for fun?"

"When I was a kid? Well, I could tell you some things that would be pretty wild, even in those days."

"And there's another angle to it," Margaret put in, saying it like a question as if she had some doubt about the assignment. "We're supposed to find out if there was some important lesson in life that you learned from some of those experiences back when you were our age."

Ace thought for a moment. He had told many yarns about a lot of people and their pranks in his day, but he had never thought of himself as a moral philosopher. "I can't say as I've ever wanted to be a preacher. That's another job I didn't fancy myself in. But I guess, now that I think of it, whenever I got into a scrape or got somebody else in one, there might be a lesson in it somewhere."

"We'd like to record the interview if you don't mind," Margaret said. "Mrs. Forbes told us we could use an empty room inside." Stilts extracted a small tape recorder from a pack he was carrying, and the little group moved into the building to a room that was almost vacant except for a table and chairs.

"What do you plan to study when you go to college?" Ace asked.

"I'm going into journalism," responded Margaret.

"I haven't decided yet," said the girl with the yellow hair. She reminded Ace of someone he had known years ago, someone whose sweet face had from time to time returned to those half-forgotten memories of an era that was fading into the misty past. For a moment Ace flashed back to the romantic days of his youth. But those times were gone now, and the present was calling.

"And what about you?" he asked the tall boy with the recorder.

"I'm going into science—some kind of science. I like experimentation."

"Well, that's good these days," Ace nodded with approval. "That reminds me that I was a scientist once. But only once, and not a real scientist, of course, just an experimenter. Maybe I could tell you a yarn about it. I haven't thought of it in years, but maybe it will give you an idea of the kind of stunts the country boys used to pull years ago." The students nodded approval, and Ace began to remember.

"It was down in Kingman, Arizona, where I was just a kid at the time. My closest friend was Andy—you'd know him if I told you who he was; he later made quite a name for himself in the movies. Well, Andy and me and one or two others hung out together quite a lot, and we was always up to some devilment and playin' tricks and things like that. Well, there was this young kid, a little younger than us, and he was always hangin' around. We didn't like him much but we couldn't get rid of him. Sometimes we'd let him tag along, though, because his folks had a great big barn that was right close to his house, and we liked to play in that barn. So in order to use the barn we'd let him play with us once in awhile.

"There was another thing about this kid that was, you might say, unusual. He was always full of wind. I never knew anybody that could—you'll pardon the expression—that could let a fart like he could. Whenever he'd break wind, you could hear it for half a mile. And the other consequences didn't improve the ventilation, either.

Well, one day we was playin' out in his barn, and he let out a big loud one. This led to some speculation about what it was that caused such a loud stink. We got real serious and scientific about it, and here's where the experiment come in.

"Ol' Andy, he says, 'That must be some kind of gas that's makin' all that noise when it escapes.' And I says, 'If it's a gas, then it ought to burn, because gas is supposed to make a fire.' And Andy says, 'Maybe some kinds of gas will burn and other kinds won't. How do we know that this kid is makin' the kind of gas that will burn? If he is, maybe we could capture it and sell it.

"Well, one thing led to another, and we decided to get a scientific experiment out of it. The kid could always tell when a big one was about to come, and of course he agreed to help us out. So the kid took off his overalls so we could get a clear shot at it when it blew, and Ol' Andy got ready with a match. Pretty soon the kid said, 'I think she's about ready to pop,' and Andy lit his match. We told the kid to bend over and let 'er go.

"Well, it was a big one, and Andy had his lit match about six inches from the kid's backside. It was gas, all right. A flame shot out of the kid like a 'cetylene torch. He let out a yell that you could hear a mile and he jumped like a cat that had been turpentined. His mother heard the ruckus, and she come chargin' out of the house to see what was the matter, and we tore out of there pretty fast, you can bet.

"Now I'd call that a true scientific experiment, and if there's any lesson to be learned from it, it might be that experimenting is all right as long as you are not the experimentee."

As Ace expected, the reaction to his story was mixed. Ted grinned as if he might have been involved in some such prank himself, Cindy giggled with amusement properly restrained by an appropriate touch of modesty, and Margaret was ready to change the subject. "That's not quite what we had in mind," she said. "What about the kind of games you used to play for amusement?"

"Oh, we played the usual kids' games like kick-the-can, run-sheep-run, prisoner's base, and such like."

It was obvious, however, that Cindy was not interested in the details of that sort of entertainment. "What about the kids, you know, boys and girls together?" she asked. "What did you do, you know, when the boys and girls would, like, have fun together?"

Ace knew exactly what she wanted to know. He thought again of a certain golden haired, round-faced girl with a smile and soft warm lips. "Oh, yes," he said, "we had plenty of kissin' games at the parties. But when we'd get out alone, maybe for a buggy ride down by the creek, or walkin' the cows home from the pasture—well, things could get a little more dangerous. But I couldn't tell you young high schoolers anything you don't already know about that. From what I've heard, you know a lot more about that kind of thing than we did then. But we had lots of parties, summer and winter, where we had a lot of fun. We'd all go swimmin' together when the weather was right—got our Saturday night bath that way—and in the winter sometimes we'd have chicken roasts.

"This was up in Utah now," Ace continued. "My folks moved up to Utah about that time, just a little country town, and we had a small gang of close friends there, boys and girls. Well, the word would go around that there was to be a chicken roast on a certain night maybe down by the willows along the creek or in an old abandoned house where there was a fireplace. Two or three of the boys would be assigned to steal one or two chickens from some neighbor's hen coop, and no one else was to know whose chickens were being swiped. It might be somebody in the gang, and of course that person was not supposed to know about it. This was always at night, of course, and the trick was to get the chicken out of that coop without upsetting all the other chickens. If that happened there was bound to be an awful squawkin' ruckus in the hen house that would bring out the farmer for sure, and sometimes he'd have a shotgun.

"Sometimes, if the folks hadn't gone to bed yet, one of the chicken stealers would knock on the door and visit with the farmer and his wife, with some excuse or other, just to keep them from hearing any possible noise in the chicken house. Then the stealer and his accomplice would take the chicken to the place where the others were waiting, and the girls would cook the chicken—usually roast it over the fire. Oh, we'd have a great time at them chicken roasts, and everybody got his turn at bein' stole from.

"Then, of course, in summer there would be melon busts, just like the chicken roasts. Every farmer had a melon patch, and he knew that sooner or later somebody would sneak in and steal a few melons. It got to be kind of a game where the farmer would try to outwit the kids. He'd plant his watermelons somewhere in a big corn field so nobody was supposed to know just where the patch was, but of course we'd always find out. Sometimes, even, the farmer would sleep on a cot out by the melon patch with a shotgun handy, and of course that always added to the excitement of it. We all had a melon patch of our own, but the fun was in stealin' some from the feller that was the most anxious not to get stole from. Those melons always tasted better if we come by 'em that way."

"You lived in the country, so did you ever play any tricks on the city kid or the stranger that would come around?" Margaret asked. "You know, like putting the tenderfoot on a wild horse like they do in the movies? Or something like a snipe hunt, where you'd have the city kid sitting out all night waiting to catch a weird creature when there wasn't any such thing."

"Oh, yes, we'd have a city kid come out once in awhile for a few weeks of country life, but they was always too smart to get caught by any snipe hunt or bronco horse. I've been bucked off plenty of times myself, but that was serious business. No, no snipe hunts in my neck of the woods. But there was one caper that would always work, and we called it Divin' for the Oysters. I'll tell you about that.

"A city kid would come out to visit somebody, and so when we weren't workin' we'd include him in whatever we might be up to at the time. When we figured the time was right, three or four of us would say, 'Let's play Divin' for Oysters.' Well, he'd naturally want to play, too, so we'd all contribute something to a kind of treasure pile—a pocket knife, a package of chewing gum, a nickel or dime—anything of some value.

"Then we'd get a wash tub and set it upside down over this pile of treasure, and then we'd review the rules so the new kid would understand the game. We were all supposed to kneel around this tub, and somebody would lift it up as quick as he could, and we were all supposed to make a dive under it, and whatever he grabbed he could keep. But before this actually happened, somebody would make an excuse to take the new kid somewhere else on an errand of some kind, and while he was out of sight one of us would go out to the pasture or corral and get the biggest, softest, greenest cow plaster he could find, and we'd take out the treasure and put that messy cow plaster under the tub.

"Then we'd bring the kid back, and we'd all get around the rub ready to grab. Somebody would count, 'One, two, three—dive!' and lift the tub. Of course, nobody but the green kid would dive for the oysters, and he'd usually go for it with both hands. He'd always come out of it a pretty mess, I can tell you, and we'd all get the laugh on him. We never learned any lesson from that, that I can think of, but you can bet the tenderfoot did."

The anecdote seemed to satisfy the young reporters. However, a second line of questioning seemed to be in their assignment, and it was Cindy's turn to bring it up. "Mr. Morgan, was there anybody in your life that you used to know, like in those old days in the West, that you would like to meet again? You know, just to find out whatever happened to them?"

Ace thought to himself, I know what you are fishing for, young lady, but I'm not about to take the bait. There was something about long golden hair, however, that stuck in his mind.

"Well, now that you mention it," he said, "there is a story that I recollect that might be what you want. Or maybe not; it doesn't shed any light on the rough-and-ready days of the West—could have happened any time, any place—but it does fit your idea that sometime in our lives we say, 'I wonder whatever happened to this or that person,' or 'I'd like to meet that person again just to put the record straight.' It'll happen to you sometime.

"I once knew a boy that told lies. He was about five or six years old at the time, and he had silky yellow hair. That was over sixty years ago, now, but I still remember that boy's hair. I was in high school then—I did get in a year or two of high school, believe it or not. This kid lived for a few months across the street from the boarding house where I stayed. He lived with his grandmother, and she was one of those excitable, domineering, unreasonable old biddies that high school boys just naturally despise.

"The first thing we noticed about the child, my high school friends and me, was that he was awful lonely. Bein' hitched up to that old lady all day long without kids of his own age to play with would naturally make him hungry for better company. So he was always running away from the hawk-eyed old woman, and he'd hang around eternally under foot where we were. We always had important things to do, but every day there he was, taggin' after us like cockleburs on a horse's tail.

"Now, most people don't know this, and you probably never thought of it yourselves, but in most teenagers there's a hidden strain of understanding and compassion—especially when it's not required or expected—for the more unfortunate of their fellow creatures. Anyway, we felt sorry for that little kid. Maybe some of us had felt a similar kind of loneliness when we were young. At any rate, we let him stick around.

"That's when we began to notice something interesting about him. His shirt and overalls were always spotlessly clean, which was a shameful condition forced upon a healthy boy by an old lady. And we also noticed his long stringy hair, which the poor old grandmother could not afford to have cut properly. We had no funds ourselves for sending the kid to the barber, so we did the next best thing. We decided to cut his hair ourselves.

"There were three or four of us involved in this caper. We propped him up in a chair in the back yard, and with all the skill of amateurs who had never cut hair before we went to work on him. We hacked and pruned and trimmed, and in spots we even scalped. We went from side to side, and we went around clockwise and counter-clockwise. We measured and sighted him in from all angles. We tried to correct our mistakes by cutting closer, but sooner or later there comes a limit even to that kind of repair job. The result was horrible.

"We finally gave up and turned the boy loose. But we told him with great emphasis that he had a very fine haircut, and he went home to his grandma as proud as could be. Of course he told her who had done this act of kindness, but she was not impressed. I think the boy got a thrashing for it.

"Naming us, I believe, was the only solid truth the boy ever told. He had an imagination big enough to accommodate a dozen normal boys. His make-believe world was as big as all outdoors. He could kill fifty robbers in one battle. Destroying monsters was merely elementary for him, and he was always breaking wild horses or diving racing cars or rescuing people from the most terrible predicaments. And at least once a day he would become a millionaire in ways that nobody could ever imagine.

"We got to enjoy the kid and his tales of miracles. His imagination deserved respect and cultivation, and we encouraged him in the use of it. We even began to speculate that he might, with this gift of exaggeration, grow up to be a great writer, or an actor, or even a politician.

"But his grandmother saw things in a different light. To her mind the boy was an outright liar. She thought those big tales of imagination could only lead him down into a life of sin and shame, and her duty was both clear and simple. She must break him of this evil practice, and she went about it in the only way she knew. She whipped him every time she caught him 'lying.' Whenever his space flights took him out of this world she would flog him back to reality. We knew this because the neighbors told us so, and we saw the marks on him.

"Then they moved away, and we never heard of them again. I never learned whatever became of that little boy. Children and dogs are forgiving creatures, and it may be that he does not carry the scars he got for his sins. It may be that he still has that gift for seeing things that aren't there and doing things that smart people know can't be done. Today, television being what it is, he might be right at home with all those monsters; he might even be successful in producing such fearsome critters for the movies.

"Or maybe he made his escape by hiding inside himself. I've seen that happen, where a person turns his back on the real world and winds up in an institution where people only pretend to agree with him. Or did he, maybe, turn out the way his grandmother thought he would? You give a dog a bad name and he'll become a bad dog, and people are like that sometimes; you give a person a bad name and he is likely to live up to it. I've often wondered which way that little boy went."

When the interview was over and the young people were going out the door it was Cindy who paused, smiled, and with a farewell wave of her hand sang a sweet "'Bye." The old man's thoughts were still more than sixty years back in time. Was there someone from his past that he would like to meet again? Not really. A pleasant memory, like a dream, can be shattered by the real light of day.

Ace Morgan was alone again. He sat on a heavy stiff-backed chair at an old table that was scarred by the marks of long use. On a shelf by the window were several tawdry pieces of craftwork fashioned by some half-talented senior citizens whose need to create still flickered in them. An hour ago Ace would have said the room was ugly—only a dismal place where old people came to express their diminishing claim to humanity before facing an uncertain but inevitable mortal destiny. But for one brief moment he saw a gleam of beauty there—a round, China-doll face, an enchanting smile, a waft of long golden hair; and he felt the intoxicating embrace of an eager young body. She would probably be a grandmother now. Maybe a great-grandmother. Perhaps the unanswered questions from the past were like the uncertainties of the future, and it was best not to know after all.

Mrs. Forbes stuck her head around the edge of the door. "Mr. Morgan," she said, "it's time to close up now."

Yes, Ace thought. It is.

Behind the Scenes

FOR THE READER who is curious about the various types of stories represented here and the techniques involved in their making, the following comments about each should prove interesting.

(The Editor)

TAMSEN DONNER'S DECISION

A story like this, based on a real-life episode in history, can be a challenge to a writer. The Donner story is of epic proportions about which whole books have been written, and to remain believably close to the facts the writer must include as much background as possible without distracting the reader from the dramatic involvement of the central character in her moments of crisis. Too much exposition would intrude on the story, but not enough would leave the plot without substance and the character without motivation.

Whether Tamsen made the right decision cannot be answered; this must be decided by the reader, whose personal attitudes will tip the balance. This reminds us that there are always two parties involved in the creation of a story, the author and the reader, who brings to it his own background of experience and values. The reader should remember, however, that Mrs. Donner was motivated by the ethical values of the 1840's and not by those of today.

The conflict centers, not around the ultimate fate of Tamsen, but the trauma of her decision and what went on in her mind. Was it a sense of atonement for a long-felt guilt, an unwavering fidelity to her marriage vows, an overpowering love for her husband, a carefully reasoned conviction that her children would find a good life without her (as indeed they did), or a private belief that the miracle of rescue would yet somehow come to her? This no one can ever know. History does record the aftermath, however; Keseberg was later rescued, but there was no sign of Mrs. Donner to be found except possibly as some bits of human remains discovered boiling in the man's cauldron.

In plot structure, there are two major crises through which the central character must pass. The second, in the scene at the lake, is less intense than the first because, while her opportunity to escape death is renewed and her agony is prolonged, the decision had already been made.

Fate, destiny, or the will of God also plays a prominent role in the story. One day might have made the difference between life or death for the main party, but for the Donners the broken axle sealed their doom. If George had died a few days sooner there would have been no decision for Tamsen to make. If Stone and Cady had been honest men the pain of her second crisis would have been avoided. And if anyone else but Keseberg had remained behind she might have been saved. The story of the ill-fated Donner Party is one of the great legends of the West, and yet parts of it are still a mystery.

REMME'S RIDE

This is a story in the tradition of a picaresque tale. While the term *picaresque* originally denoted a form of literature in which the hero was a rogue whose adventures were described in a series of episodes, it can also be applied to the adventures of a character who is not a rogue but whose exploits or difficulties occur along the road. In this case the hazards constitute a test of a man's strength, resolution, and endurance as he proceeds from one point to another.

His initial motivation is believable. Anyone finding himself in similar circumstances would do everything he could to recoup his losses, particularly if his failure meant total ruin. His struggle is against a variety of forces, and we are interested in the sequence of crises along the road—the changing nature of his obstacles and their increasing intensity. The reader wants him to succeed, and the suspense is gradually increased by two elements operating concurrently: the gradual diminishing of his endurance, and the fact that even if he should reach his destination he could lose the race with the ship which is speeding toward Portland.

The ship does not appear in the story except in Remme's mind, but it is nevertheless a real threat of which the reader is reminded from time to time. The inciting incident in the plot is the bank failure, but a logical solution of the problem—that of finding another branch of the bank—is impossible. Remme must then seek a less rational course of action. Having set forth upon his bold adventure, he faces obstacles that test different aspects of his character, starting with the temptation of the widow Elkins.

His next crisis shifts from human opposition to that of nature. Lost in a wilderness where snow has obliterated the trail, he still has his wits about him, and he uses an element of nature, the instincts of the horse, to overcome the trick of nature. He is still using his head when he lies to Elisha Steele to obtain a fresh horse. Then nature again becomes his adversary when he almost freezes to death in the mountain storm. (It is not part of this story, but historians may note the ironic fact that several years later he did meet his death in a storm in these very same mountains.)

He is saved from the next possible disaster by having a horse that can outrun the Indians. Then his opposition shifts to fatigue within himself. Both mind and body are beginning to fail him. Ultimately, with his wits restored, he is able to win his game, but the nemesis of chance pursues him to the very last moment of his contest. Both Remme and the reader escape from the spell at the same time.

THE BODEGA WAR

The reader might wish to ask whether this is a story predominantly of plot or of character. According to historians such a "land war" actually occurred, but simply recounting events does not make a short story. In terms of plot, the controlling factor in the action is the law in a conflict between property rights and personal rights, and the question of what is or should be legal serves as a kind of thread to which the action is tied and which links the motivation of the three principal characters. Curtis maintains that the law must be upheld; Terry sees it as an instrument of injustice to be resisted; and the sheriff finds it to be a disturbing complication that somehow must be avoided.

The story ends at its climax, the highest point of plot action, and what follows this is the denouement, or the final solution. This may seem like an anti-climax or "let down" for the story, but to have the outcome told in three different versions is a device that not only explains "how it came out" but also completes the character delineation of each of the three participants. Curtis can claim victory by acknowledging the social responsibility forced upon him. Terry can claim victory by having achieved for the settlers ownership of the land in a way that is ultimately legal. And the sheriff, though a coward at heart, can claim victory by exaggerating the facts.

Some readers, however, may see this as primarily a story of character. The two opposing protagonists are revealed as men of strength and determination, and the impression is created that neither will yield, yet in the end both have to compromise. Their avowed unwillingness to give in, therefore, is modified at last by reason and good sense. The ironic social commentary here is that the sheriff, a man who has sworn to uphold the law, is the coward, yet he can make himself appear as a hero. Although his version of the story is farthest from the truth, it is the one that is most likely to be remembered in western legendry.

In each of the three characters there are contradictions, some physical and some psychological. The sheriff is a fat man with no guts. Curtis is a realist, but with a mistaken sense of his own power, and consequently he chooses the wrong way to solve his problem. Terry is an idealist with an Irish gift of persuasion that leads him into an impossible situation without regard for the possible consequences. Even when Curtis realizes that matters have gone beyond his control, he boldly maintains his bluff. Terry knows that his emotional boasting has led the settlers to expect more than he can deliver, when in fact he has actually promised them nothing except the chance through their mob instincts to relieve their frustrations. In the ultimate confrontation, therefore, like Curtis he can only bluff. And the sheriff is caught between two opposing forces with which he cannot cope; the situation that he is expected to control has been out of hand from the beginning.

The theme of this story has modern implications. It is by law, reason, diplomacy, and compromise that crucial differences are settled, not by open warfare.

LUCIA AND OLD LACE

There is a minimum of dialogue in this story; it is mostly exposition, so we therefore must interpret the character of Lucia by what she does. She is an intelligent and resourceful girl who is caught up in the patriotic zeal of the Old South in the Civil War. Being the only girl in a family with five brothers, she wants to emulate them by doing what she can do best—use her brains and her feminine wiles, which is a stereotype characteristic of Southern ladies of the period. The ordeal of being a spy, however, is a disintegrating force in her life. She is constantly in peril and the stakes are high, a matter of life and death. The danger increases to a point beyond endurance and she must find deliverance.

Ironically, however, just as her release is at hand she is discovered, and her career ends in frantic despair. She is the victim of a blighted life, with failure at every turn through no direct fault of her own. Her motivating cause, to defend the aristocratic way of life in the ante-bellum South, became futile when the South lost the War. Her brothers died in the War. Her discovered identity in San Francisco ended her career. She had given up the possibility of love and happiness, and like Scarlett O'Hara she became obsessed with the protection of her property for the sake of security.

The lace stole, which was the one symbol of elegance, beauty, and gracious living, remains with her; but in a final act of despair she sacrifices that. We know, then, that she has completely surrendered and needs to obliterate the past and everything that might signify old dreams. It is a symbolic act of spiritual suicide. What happens after that is a long prison term, figuratively speaking, that can only end in frustration and death. In this regard, therefore, she epitomizes the dying splendor and the vanquished hopes of the Old South.

In terms of technique, the story begins near the climax, with a flashback to explain events leading up to that point. This captures the reader's interest immediately, and the background facts then become more relevant. The three or four scenes revealed in detail, as if a motion picture "camera eye" were focusing in, mark the points of crisis in the story. The plot climax (which does not always coincide with the emotional climax of a story) comes in the scene at the Presidio when her identity is discovered, but the emotional climax is not reached until she destroys her lace and other memorabilia. What happens after that is merely the "denouement," or a rapid conclusion or aftermath. It is a tragic story of unrealized ideals and vanquished dreams.

THE MINK CREEK GHOST

The story of the ghost of Mink Creek is a local legend still being told, and this is only one version. There is horror in what happens, but for the reader there is not much suspense; he can guess what is going to happen after the first dramatic crisis is revealed. The three violent deaths are simply one episode repeated without any rise in intensity or apprehension. And as far as the plot is concerned, the futile attempts of the townspeople to avert a repetition of the tragedy do not really foreshadow any likelihood of success unless the reader brings to the story a belief that ardent prayer will triumph over evil.

The characters are for the most part only shadowy figures. The Olsons, the dog, the mother, and the girls have no real personalities; they are merely stick figures manipulated through the plot. Mr. Burrell is seen more clearly as a person, so it is upon him that the action of the story must depend for motivation.

But if this is not a story of either plot or character, what is it that has made it endure as a legend and makes it interesting as a short story? It is the overwhelming power of evil at work, invisibly, relentlessly, and inescapably. It is the repugnant mystery of it that intrigues the folk and gives the occurrence the life of a legend, and it is the fascination we all have with the presence of forces we cannot understand or explain that holds the reader.

It is not natural forces that are at work here, and we are teased by the need to find an explanation. Some might say that there can be enough psychic power generated through imagination and fear, when it is concentrated in time, place, and situation, to produce such kinetic manifestations. History records many cases in which the "demon syndrome," which allows evil spirits to possess human beings and dominate their thoughts and actions, sometimes with violent and disastrous effects. So if one can speculate on the possibility that unseen evil spirits can take over and do things beyond the reach of our knowledge or reason, then what happens at Mink Creek becomes a real story.

The conclusion of the narrative may be disappointing if we expect a plausible explanation. The double murder and the killing of the dog may validate the concentration of guilt in Mr. Burrell, but they do not explain—beyond the fact that they make the events possible—the intervention of vengeful ghosts or evil demons. The success of the story, therefore, depends upon its vivid descriptions, which bring the reader into the scene, and the awareness that superstition can become a powerful force in the lives of people who fear the devil.

UNTO HER A CHILD WAS BORN

A good short story is supposed to achieve a single narrative effect with the greatest economy of means consistent with the utmost emphasis. Sometimes, however, a story will create two thematic impressions if one tends to reinforce the other. This is the case in "Unto Her a Child Was Born." It is first a Christmas story in which two young boys are at the borderline between childhood and adulthood, and we see them trying to cling to the illusions of a child's faith in the literal Christchild story in resistance to the realities of an adult world. But it is also a character sketch of a small community which is faced with the intrusion of outside-world reality into their idyllic and tranquil microcosm of traditional moral values.

In both sets of characters adjustment is called for. Here the townspeople are mature enough to make the adjustment without conflict. In most fiction it is assumed that the small town with a religious background would show a bigoted attitude and a narrow-minded intolerance for the symbol of sin in their midst. The reader may be surprised, therefore, to find that this town is different. The rustic wisdom of Mr. Stowe and Homer's stepfather validates the attitude of the town. And Uncle George represents the community's roots in the past and the sterling pioneer virtues of practicality, romantic idealism, and intolerance that can override prejudice; and the young boys of the second or third generation, by their closeness to him, show their willingness to carry on such traditions. These rustic people live close to the earth and know how strong the forces of nature are within human beings.

For the boys, this acceptance of nature is also basic, but they have an additional fascination with the condition of Rebecca. Christmas is coming and a child is coming. The two events must have some mysterious connection. While they are united in their desire to cling to Christmas as a miraculous experience, however, they have different personalities and will grow up to be different types of persons. Homer is the realist. He willingly joins in the making of a gift, which is a good thing to do, but he doubts the possibility of miracles in his own town. With a realistic respect for facts, he casts doubt on Earl's fantasies.

Earl, on the other hand, is still living in imagination. He incites the action and resists disillusionment until the very end. The theme of the story, therefore, is that however ardently we may cling to the make-believe world of childhood, the time comes when we must grow up and accept things as they really are. Our evolving role in the Christmas ritual as we grow up reflects such a crisis in everyone's life.

DEATH VALLEY SCOTTY

In the strict sense of the word, this is not a short story but a biographical sketch. The object here is to reveal the facts in a flamboyant character's life, and since Scotty was a real person we are interested in the documented events which made him what he was or what he seemed to be. The sketch must therefore be more expository than narrative. He is an extraordinary person who became a legend in California, a legend created and nurtured by himself. And as in most legends, facts and fiction often become indistinguishable.

To provide a narrative framework for the catalog of biographical data, this piece resorts to the whimsical device of taking him out of real life and catching him at a point where all the fragments must come together. The beginning and end, therefore, are out of this world. This trick was used satirically by Lord Byron in his "The Vision of Judgment," and if it succeeds here the reader can enjoy a look at Scotty in a place where only the truth matters.

If there is a theme in this sketch, it is the same as that which guided Scotty through life: that people must enjoy being fooled; otherwise, they would not be so eager to take the fast-deal artist's bait.

Some scholars believe that California's three most popular and representative legends are the stories about Joaquin Murieta, The Donner Party, and Death Valley Scotty. If they are right, this sketch will epitomize the youngest of the three, and it will continue as long as Scotty's Castle endures. More material about Scotty can be found in Earl C. Driskill, *Death Valley Scotty Rides Again* (Death Valley: Earl C. Driskill, 1955); I.B. Beldon, *Mines of Death Valley* (Glendale: La Siesta Press, 1966); and Hank Johnson, *The Man and the Myth, Death Valley Scotty* (Yosemite: Flying Spur Press, 1972).

Other good references are W. A. Chalfant, *Death Valley, The Facts* (Stanford University Press, 1930, 1936); C. B. Glasscock, *Here's Death Valley* (New York: Grosset & Dunlap, 1940); and Dorothy Shally and William Bolton, *Scotty's Castle* (Yosemite: Flying Spur Press, 1973).

It has been said of Scotty, "He was a man of great integrity—lied only when it was best for everyone or would cause a roar from the crowd." Somehow this reminds us of a wise saying by Mark Twain: "The truth is such a rare commodity, we should be sparing in our use of it."

DOWN THE HOLE

In this story the central character is confronted with two powerful and conflicting forces. His background of poverty intensifies his motivation to earn enough money to return to school, but this initially secure line of action is jeopardized by an embarrassingly mundane kind of accident which threatens his security and leads to a very dangerous experience. His first conflict is an ethical one, but his need is stronger than his sense of morality and he decides to endure the pain, danger, and the risk of discovery in order to have the mining company pay for his ultimate security.

Symbolically, the elements of the story portend death. The accident occurs when night is approaching. The skies darken as he makes his journey to the "hole," which is a kind of hell. The gathering storm portends disaster as the hostility of nature becomes a threat to his enterprise. He meets his friend Art, who represents the temporary intrusion of realism and life into his journey toward the hole, which is uphill all the way, but even the unwelcome presence of Art superimposes the vision of death upon the realities of life.

The ride into the mine is a symbolic journey into death. The increasing danger adds suspense to the story, as does the painful strain on the young man's physical endurance. Once under ground he is supported more by his instincts than reason. His boss Baxter becomes a kind of Pluto, a god of

the underworld, who has the power to give or take away the resources
sought by the central character. In terms of the narrative plot, the turning
point comes when the ruse succeeds and the character is returned to the
outer world, but as an allegory the story must continue. Symbolically,
therefore, the character returns to life after his crisis, and the subsequent
threats to his future success become minor ones.

What follows afterward might seem anti-climactic, but in real life the
return to normality is usually an anti-climax. The symbolism continues:
the town wakes up from its night of sleep and the routine activities of life
are resumed. Likewise, the young man's life is restored to its normal ebb
and flow, as indicated by his naturally aroused interest in the young girl
who attends him. The universality of the theme then becomes clear; the
young man is a surrogate for the reader or anyone who has passed
through a crisis. He is given no name in the story because he is Everyman.

The ethical question raised in the beginning finds its own answer. As
in real life, an act of doubtful morality which proves successful and
advantageous is usually buried and easily forgotten or excused.

THE CELEBRATED MILLARD COUNTY
DRAMATIC STOCK COMPANY

This mock-heroic saga provides a good example of how the point of view
from which it is told can affect the narrative impression of a story. If it
were told from the usual external, third-person, objective point of view, it
would become a satirical and somewhat demeaning account of the
misadventures of amateurs deluded by unrealistic dreams of grandeur. But
by having these accidents recounted with tongue-in-cheek seriousness by
one of the participants, the story becomes humorous without any "put-
downs." In other words, we can laugh with a person who reveals the
innocence of his own kind by telling a joke about himself.

We find no elaborated character sketches developed here. Mr. Rasmussen, Lillian, Dr. Baker, and the narrator are really only types, though
taken together as a troupe each adds a small portion to the character of the
group as a whole. The exception, of course, is Byron, who does emerge as
a personality. He wants to perform magic but doesn't get the chance. Yet
he plays the role of a magician for this little company by mixing the unreal
with the real, fantasy with fact. He can dream of fame in Hollywood and
even imagine himself with an elegant name to fit a new identity, and he
can keep the hopes of the group alive after each discouragement. He fails
every time, as reality checkmates each hope, yet he is needed in the story
as an identifiable link to splice the episodes together. It is his wit that

keeps the farce moving from crisis to crisis. Byron may fail, but he is never defeated, and in the end we see him going off to the university to pursue another dream.

GOING HOME

Most readers will probably find this to be a very sad story. Certainly there is pathos here, but whether or not it could be called tragic depends on the extent to which the reader can identify with the central character, a man once successful in his own field who fails through no fault of his own. It is about the defeat and disintegration that befell so many persons rendered helpless during the depression of the 1930's.

In this story everything is out of joint. Hemphill is a displaced person, the people at the boarding house live twisted and frustrated lives, and the dominating optimism of Ma Canfield defies reality. Even the style in which the story is told is deliberately distorted; sometimes the reader is inside the mind of Hemphill, and at other times an external view depicts actual scenes and dialogue just outside the borderline of his consciousness.

The imagery symbolizes futility, disintegration, and death. The metaphor of a corner is first intellectually considered, and then gradually it becomes a figurative trap in which the central character is caught. Likewise, the "end of the line" becomes a recurring image. First, Hemphill goes as far west as he can, to the end of the road across the continent, and then the end of the streetcar line picks up the figurative refrain. Finally the end of life becomes literally the end of the line. Also threaded through the story is another set of images, with the dead leaves swirled by the wind, the uprooted and decaying tumbleweeds, the discarded Christmas trees and wrappings symbolizing winter in which all things must die.

In tone the story is ironic. The devices Hemphill tries to sell are supposed to bring security to his customers; what he himself needs most in life, he is trying to make available to others. Also ironic is the fact that while he is selling shoes to people who can afford them, his own soles are wearing out. And the man with the good job, the typesetter, who is the only one capable of helping Hemphill, gambles away his money. And the ultimate irony is that Hemphill has his wish granted, to go home.

The direction in which the plot unfolds is also subject to the caprices of fate. Although the character is pushed gradually and inevitably toward defeat, he is taunted with occasional flashes of hope which give the story an up and down movement, yet he never really overcomes the obstacles that bar his way. The thematic conclusion is foreshadowed in the anonymous headpiece that precedes the narrative—a man has lost his identity completely.

THE LEGEND OF CHIEF LITTLE SITTING BEAR

This is a "first-person" story, but we can assume that it is really true and not merely told in the first person for effect. Its theme is that the folk can triumph over the establishment. Told with tongue-in-cheek humor, it is also a mild satire on the traveling public, who are usually more interested in entertainment than facts. Many guides, tour directors and even ranger-naturalists in the National Parks used to embellish their information with fanciful and imaginative anecdotes not intended to deceive but to entertain.

From the beginning it is clear that the narrator is part of an established system, and with good humor he is looking for ways to express his individuality in what could otherwise become a monotonous routine. Since the vacationers are also shedding the monotony in their lives, he shares a closer relationship with his audiences than does the "management" of the National Park.

We can assume that the two naturalists in the story are scientists qualified for their jobs, but with mock-seriousness this aspect of their real duties is minimized to the level of the fanciful tale of Chief Little Sitting Bear. And the Indian tale itself is so patently trite and sentimental that no one is really expected to believe it. But it does give the public what they enjoy hearing as a romantic relief from all the "authentic" facts they have been given. If the naturalists had been allowed to repeat this tale throughout the season to hundreds of people, it probably would have found its way into "the literature" along with other such Indian romances. If this had happened, however, these rangers would be in trouble with the folklore scholars, who disapprove of making up synthetic or bogus folklore. Such creations they call "fakelore."

With minor adjustments this yarn would be successful in the arena of oral storytelling.

ON BECOMING SOMEBODY

The whole point of this story is its theme. The narrator is not a character; he is merely an observer and to some degree a catalyst. And if the reader is looking for scenic descriptions or plot conflicts, they are not here. The struggle is internal and implied rather than expressed.

At first glance the character of Joe may seem to be two-dimensional, and as in a morality play the philosophical message may appear to overbalance the plot. A closer look, however, will reveal Joe's third dimension, which lies beneath the surface. He is caught at a turning point in his life, and the reader—who observes this through the professor's eyes—can infer what is going on in Joe's mind. We learn with the narrator that the external image is not the real Joe.

The fact that he had rejected his mother and was trying to assume the role of a rugged character who could attract attention by being abrasive, suggests that he was searching for an identity with which he could live. He had fooled his professors and was deluding himself, and inwardly he suspected this. All the time he had within him a vulnerability, as evidenced by his reaction to the story of the Polish couple, and he wanted a better reason than he had been able to find to accept the heritage that was his birthright. It took the Polish story to crack the emotional barrier and break the shell that he had constructed, but he was still unsure. He still had to test the validity of his hidden identify. He was testing when he cautiously and somewhat doubtfully agreed to collect his mother's songs. He was still testing when he submitted himself to the graduation exercises which he had previously rejected, and when he kept his mother hidden until she could be accepted by the professor, who represented values he did respect.

When his mother was recognized and honored as a precious link with his cultural birthright, his doubts were resolved; he had found out who he was. The jigsaw pieces fell into place for him, and he was ready to go on and complete the picture of himself that unconsciously he had always wanted to find.

To some degree every young person must resolve the same conflict. Consequently, the appeal of this story is not merely to those who have an interest in ethnic problems; it is really directed to all of humanity and particularly to those who can feel the emotional impact of seeing a fellow soul in conflict. The reader should realize, therefore, that this is not two stories, but one; the story within the story about the Polish couple is only a means to an end, a motivating force that gives Joe the strength to break out of his prison.

THE SLAVES OF STONEY CREEK

Historians know the basic facts about the capture of many Indians and their virtual enslavement at the early-day California missions. The motives for such practices, of course, depended on different points of view. For some, the need for labor was real and the enslavement of Indians was profitable. Others, however, believed that the opportunity to "civilize" them and save their souls through the white man's religion justified the policy. That this happened is well recorded, but the point of view of the victims is seldom considered from the human and emotional level of the Indians themselves.

Here, then, is a true personal narrative about one such episode that was first told by an Indian. The author wants it to be heard, however, not as an immediate first-person account, but as an echo from long ago. The problem in achieving this effect, therefore, is one of style. An image of the old woman is first established through the memory of her grandson, to whom the tale was told. She is ancient, and so is her story. Obviously she spoke in a dialect that was a mixture of Indian, Mexican, and English, but an attempted imitation of such speech would get in the way of the story. As the narrative shifts, therefore, from the opening character sketch of old Maria to the plot action involving the slaves, its cadence and imagery must change, but only enough to suggest the Indian origin without over-flavoring the style.

But style is only the means to an end. The basic question should be what is the single narrative effect that stays in one's mind after reading the story. Is this predominantly a story of character or theme? One reader may see it as the portrayal of Maria and Antonio as persons who never lose hope and have the strength to survive through adversity. Another reader may see this in terms of its theme, in which the effect is an expression of a universal truth, that everyone has an unquenchable need to be free, and the uplifing lesson that we can make the best of misfortune and always remain true to our own identity. Whether this moral is merely a banal platitude or is believably developed from the experiences recounted here, that is for the reader to decide.

THERE COULD BE A LESSON IN IT SOMEWHERE

This is a character sketch rather than a short story in the usual sense. For a brief moment Ace Morgan is allowed to expose three different aspects of his character: as an ordinary senior citizen not unlike others about whom he can make ironically critical remarks; as a prankish lad from a long-gone era of the past, and again one of a group representing a segment of rural life; and finally as an individual with memories that show a deeper sense of humanity than most older people are seldom given credit for having.

In a short story or sketch, a character cannot grow and develop, as happens in the longer genre of the novel; he can only be revealed in a moment of exposure as having traits that are already within him. So with

Ace; not only the different aspects of his personality are disclosed, but also the sequence of these glimpses, the order of progression, becomes important.

First he is a satirical jokester with a reputation for spinning yarns. He clearly understands that he is part of a group with nothing to talk about but their memories, and he can make fun of himself as well as his fellow seniors. But he is led out of this pose by the serious interest of the high school students in something more meaningful in life. We learn through this device that the yarnspinner Ace is but an external image, and contrary to his own denials he has deeper values in life. The episode about the little boy who told lies reveals this. His philosophy is neither profound nor abstract, but it shows him as a sensitive and compassionate person.

The third disclosure of his character, his return to the memory of a long lost romance, does not make him unique but rather as one whose youthful experiences are universal; every older person can re-awaken such sleeping memories. It is the golden hair and the tempting grace of the young girl that serves as a leitmotif in the sketch; it lures him into a hidden corner of his past, his early—perhaps his first—romance; and it also triggers his anecdote about the little boy, which gives him a way to avoid acknowledging that Cindy has reminded him of his youth.

If this sketch has a theme, it might be that older people are too often underrated: that they have taken chances, enjoyed blissful romances, performed acts of tenderness, and learned important lessons from life. There is sadness, too, in the fact that in our society they are eventually discarded, and that too often it takes an assignment of some kind to bring the old and the young together where they can meet on an equal plane.